MW00639139

THE REBEL

EMERSON PASS HISTORICALS
BOOK EIGHT

TESS THOMPSON

Copyright © 2023 by Tess Thompson

All rights reserved.

No part of this book may be reproduced in any form or by any electronic or mechanical means, including information storage and retrieval systems, without written permission from the author, except for the use of brief quotations in a book review.

❀ Created with Vellum

THE REBEL

This one is for all the loyal and enthusiastic fans of Emerson Pass. Your emails and messages mean so much to me. Thank you for making it all the way to end of the Barnes family saga. Sending love to you and yours from the bottom of my weird little author heart.

1

DELPHIA

On a frosty morning in early December, the train I'd taken from the east rounded the last corner before Emerson Pass. I breathed a sigh of relief. This was the last stop on a long journey home. My stomach fluttered with excitement. I would see my family at last. Perhaps even Jack would be there to greet me. At the thought of Jack, I pulled my compact from my purse to check my lipstick. Bright red, as was the fashion, and none on my teeth. My hair looked as good as was possible after many days on the train. I stuck a pin through my derby hat to secure it better and then put my powder away.

The train shuddered to a stop. I rubbed my finger against the glass, making a circle with which to peer out to the platform. What I saw surprised me a great deal. Or should I say, what I didn't see? No one was there. Not a single person stood on the platform. No bodies milled about inside where it was most likely warmer, either.

Where was my family? When one of our own returned from an adventure, the Barnes family came to welcome them home. I'd expected that all of my six siblings, their spouses, and my

1

nieces and nephews would be there, waving and smiling, my mother crying with joy at seeing me. We were a large, messy clan that had weathered many trials and celebrated many joyous occasions. My coming home after four years at university was supposed to be one of the latter. Instead, the station seemed strangely still, as if it had been frozen in time, as in a fairy tale. The fir and pine trees were covered with a fresh layer of snow. Ice made the leafless aspens look like finely spun sugar. From the look of the white sky, snow would soon fall again.

A shiver of worry sped up my spine. Was something wrong?

There was no one else in the passenger car. Not many ventured this far into the Rockies, and most had gotten off at the stop for Louisville, a bigger town at a much lower elevation than Emerson Pass.

I took my valise from under my seat and steadied myself. There was nothing wrong. They'd gotten the date and time mixed up. That was all. Perhaps they thought I was coming home tomorrow? Today, the seventh of December, was a Sunday. Had my mother been confused, thinking I would come Monday instead? She was not one to get details muddled, especially when the baby of the family returned back to the nest.

What if someone was sick in the family?

Please, God, don't let it be Papa.

He was in his mid-sixties now, and although he was as robust and energetic as he'd always been, I worried. My mother was almost fifteen years his junior. The thought of either of them being without the other was impossible for me to even imagine. Their love story was one for the ages.

I glanced down at the gold watch my parents had given me for my graduation from Bryn Mawr last spring. I'd graduated with a degree in mathematics. Not typical for a woman, I'd heard more than once, but I didn't care. I loved every minute of my studies and had tutored half a dozen of my girlfriends to help them pass their classes. The joy I felt in teaching, seeing the delight on their faces when they finally understood a concept, inspired me to think about becoming a professor myself.

After graduation, I'd been offered a job as an assistant to a math professor at Harvard. After some time, in combination with a good recommendation, I could go on to graduate school. I'd lasted six months with my pig of a boss before coming to my senses. Not only did he treat me like a secretary instead of a mathematician, but one day, as I leaned over his desk to retrieve a piece of paper he wanted, he'd put his hand up my skirt. I suspect it was my hard kick to his male region, one that left him writhing on the floor, that led to my immediate dismissal. I smiled, remembering his howls of pain as I stomped out of his office, never to return.

Which now left me feeling like an accomplished young woman, home after graduating with honors. As much as I'd thought a life in academia was what I wanted, it was not to be.

Anyway, I wanted to be home with my family. I'd already missed four years of my nieces' and nephews' birthdays and graduations. In addition, my closest sister, Addie, had her first novel based on our family published with great success. She'd taken the stories the others had told us growing up and put them into a novel about the five Carrow children. There were all sorts of scrapes and high jinks and family love. I'd cried my eyes out over every scene when I'd read the final edition. I'd been her very first reader from the very first draft, yet I couldn't help but be drawn into the story as if I were reading it all for the first time. I filled with pride just thinking of it all now.

Despite her success, she'd remained humble and as sweet as she'd always been. James, who was now the principal at the high school, as well as teaching all the English courses, had been overjoyed at her triumph. He'd once been an editor in New York and knew a thing or two about books and writers. Without his encouragement, I don't know if my sister would have had the courage to send her novel out to editors. All that was history now. She was now a successful author.

In addition to all that, there was a job waiting for me here. One I could excel in. I hoped I would, anyway. Papa had offered me a position in his company, working under my brother Flynn and brother-in-law Phillip. When I'd come home for Christmas last, they all tried to convince me to come home right after graduation; however, they'd understood I wanted to try my hand in academia instead. But if I wanted a job in the family business, it would be here when I was ready. Well, the time had come. I was ready all right.

I stepped into the frigid air. The tip of my nose went cold as I scanned the platform. Silence met me. Even the ticket master was missing, and the window of his booth closed.

Clutching my valise, I walked toward the inside of the station. If no one had come for me, it would be best to wait inside where it was warm. I'd no sooner walked through the door and inhaled a breath of warm air than I saw Jack Depaul sprinting toward the front doors.

My pulse quickened at the sight of him. He wore a pair of denim jeans, a plaid shirt, and a cowboy hat perched on top of his perfect head, hiding his thick dark hair. I knew that head of hair like the back of my fingertips. I blushed, remembering how I'd run my fingers through his hair all those years ago after our graduation from high school and then kissed him right on the mouth and told him, "I've been wanting to do that for so long." He'd stared at me with wide eyes, obviously discombobulated by my brazen advances. The next day, I'd blamed it on the clandestine spiked punch one of my girlfriends had given me at the bonfire. That devil juice had made me bold. I'd never in my life done something like it and never had again. Jack was the only boy I'd ever kissed. To this day, the memory was still fresh four and a half years later. As was the desire to do it again.

We'd laughed it off at the time, blaming that silly punch. We

4

were best friends, nothing more, he'd said. "Best not to get any notions in our heads, what with you leaving at the end of the summer." I cringed even now, thinking about how humiliated I'd been. He clearly had not felt what I had.

Since then, I'd seen Jack on holidays, more from afar than up close. Busy helping his father run their horse farm, he had little time for entertainment. By the time I came back for the summer between my freshman and sophomore years, he had a girlfriend. Helen. Flaxen-haired Helen from Denver, who wore fashionable clothes and sparkly jewelry. The daughter of a horse trader. What could be more perfect for Jack? My sister Fiona said they'd met during an auction. She must be something, I'd thought at the time, to snatch up Jack Depaul. When I'd seen her with my own eyes, I'd understood only too well her appeal to the rougher sex.

So that was that, I'd told myself. What did I expect? That he would wait around for me while I finished school when he hadn't wanted me in the first place? I'd been the only one of us to feel a stirring so deep that it competed with the idea of college. If he'd said he felt the same way, I might not have gone to school. A terrible mistake that would have been, I reminded myself now as I took in the pure masculinity of the man as he strode through the doors of the station, yanking his hat from his head.

Regardless, growing up and even now, he was a person I greatly admired. He was kind but also smart. Strong as an ox, the man could work harder and longer than anyone I'd ever witnessed. He and his brother, Henry, had been working on their father's horse farm since they could walk. As far as I could tell, he loved his horses and that land more than he'd ever love a woman. I supposed I should pity Helen. What a trial it would be to marry a man like Jack. One would always be second to the horses.

That said, as far as I knew, they weren't yet engaged. Maybe she'd given up on him? Otherwise, why hadn't they married yet? I didn't want to ask Addie or Mama about him for fear I'd give myself away. Like many things in life, I knew what I could have and what I couldn't. Jack Depaul was as hard to tame as one of his young horses, and apparently, I wasn't the one to do so. Lucky Helen, I thought as I gazed into his deep blue eyes.

He held his hat in front of him, looking much too good. No man should be this virile and handsome. It was enough to unsteady the steadiest of women, namely me. "Delphia Barnes. Aren't you a sight for sore eyes? You look as beautiful as ever. Welcome home."

"It's nice to see you too. Where's everyone else?"

He looked at me blankly, as if he hadn't heard my question correctly. "I'm sorry it's just me here to fetch you, but considering everything, no one wanted to leave the house."

I clutched the handle of my valise so hard my fingers hurt. "Did something happen to my father?"

"No, no, nothing like that." He ran a hand through his thick hair and looked up at the ceiling. "You haven't heard the news. Obviously, you haven't."

"What news?"

"The Japanese bombed Pearl Harbor early this morning. They blew up the *Arizona* and the *Shaw*."

"What?"

"Those are navy ships stationed at Pearl Harbor. We lost thousands of men on the *Arizona*. Thousands." His voice sounded as dull as his eyes looked. "Everyone's home listening to the radio, hoping for more news. We'll join the war. We have no choice after this."

I nodded. For months now, the debate about whether we should join the Allies had occupied much of the American consciousness. People had views on either side. I'd hoped we could stay out of it. I had seen close up what the first war had done to my brother Theo. He and Flynn had fought in the Great

War, and he'd come home haunted by what he'd seen and done. Why did there have to be another one? Now we would be in it, no question.

Instinctively, I clutched his arm. "I don't want us to fight. Can't we just leave it be?"

"Not after they went after our people. I expect Roosevelt will make an announcement soon."

"But we've already gone through the Depression. Wasn't that bad enough?" So many had suffered since the crash. Would we have more suffering? Hadn't our generations seen enough hardship?

"Yes, but we can't let them get away with killing Americans. There were civilians killed, too. We have to fight."

I quickly ran through how many young men in our family were of the age to fight. My nephews, Bleu and Beaumont, were my age. They'd been adopted by Fiona and Li when they were eight. Ironically, they'd brought them over from France. Were they fated to return? Only this time in American uniforms? Louisa and Theo's son Simon wouldn't be quite old enough yet, but next year he would be. And what about Jack?

My knees weakened at the thought of those sweet young men sent to a war that should have nothing to do with us.

He smiled down at me. "What a way to greet you. Once again, welcome home."

"How come you came to get me?" I'm of average height, but next to this large man, I felt demure and petite.

"I brought a colt over for your dad this morning. We heard the news together and were unable to tear ourselves away from the reports. I offered to come get you so they could stay to hear whatever comes next."

"That was nice of you." I realized I was still holding onto his arm. Self-conscious, I let go while continuing to look up at him. "You look good. As always."

"Thanks. Hard work keeps a man fit." He grinned that

devilish grin of his. Did the man get better looking every year? "I'm honored to be the one to welcome you back home. I still can't believe you're here. I thought I'd never see you again once you started your career in academia."

"It wasn't for me, actually."

"Your father mentioned something about the man you were working for and his ungentlemanly behavior. I hope you hurt him good." His blue eyes twinkled. Such long, thick lashes for a man. It must be his French heritage. His father had emigrated from France with his parents and little sister, Poppy.

"Yes, it was quite satisfying," I said. "But somewhat career-ending."

"Their loss is our gain. Is this your only bag?" Jack asked, indicating my suitcase.

I looked down at my bag. "Yes, I sent the rest through the post."

"Are you really home for good?" His eyes searched my face. Was there a weight to his question?

"I am. The boys want me to run the nightclub. They're tired of it. Or their wives are, anyway." My oldest sister, Josephine, was married to Phillip. He helped my brother Flynn run the lodge and nightclub, as well as designed and built furniture on the side. Jo said he was too busy all the time and worn out from all his duties. "And Mama approves now that booze is legal again."

"It's been for a while now," Jack said, chuckling.

"I know, much to my mother's dismay."

He gestured toward the parking lot. "May I carry your bag for you?"

"Like you used to in school?" When we were in high school together, he used to pick me up for school in his dad's old truck and insisted on carrying my books into the building.

"Those were fun days, weren't they?" His tone bordered on wistful. "I've missed them. And you."

"Really?" I had such fond memories of those days, bouncing around in the cab of his truck, talking about horses and music, and whatever else came to mind. We'd been such good friends back then. Until I ruined it for myself by falling for him. Never again, though. He was taken, and it was best I remember that.

"Why wouldn't I?" Jack asked. "You were my best friend when we were kids. That doesn't change just because you're a fancy city girl now."

"I'm not a city girl. Take it back." I smacked his chest.

He laughed and caught my hand, holding it against his chest for a moment. "We missed you around here, Delphia Barnes. It's been a little less interesting around here without you. Quite a bit less interesting."

"Well, here I am. About to make things interesting."

He let go of my hand but not before saying, "Of that, I have no doubt."

I stole a glance at his hand as he picked up my suitcase. No ring. I would have heard if he'd gotten married. Maybe they were still engaged? Or had they broken up? I would ask him, I decided, once we were in the car.

To my delight, he was driving his old truck. He tossed my bag in the back and then opened the passenger door for me. "You remember this old pile of metal?" Jack asked, reaching for my hand to help me jump up and into the interior.

"Sure. I loved this old girl. She's holding up fine."

"Some girls get better with age." He grinned before shutting the door. I watched as he sprinted around the front of the truck. How was he out in this weather without an overcoat? Not that I minded. I enjoyed the way his flannel shirt clung to his muscular chest. I'd felt those muscles when he'd twirled me around the dance floor back in high school. Although we'd never been a couple, he'd always been the one to take me to dances. He was the best dancer in our class. I always felt like a princess in his arms.

When he got in, he started the truck, which roared to life with a rumble and a shake. Gasoline wafted into the cabin. "Sorry about the smell," Jack said with a grimace.

"I like it," I said.

He laughed. "That right?"

"Reminds me of you." Why had I said that? I wanted to clap my hand over my mouth. What a ninny.

The corners of his mouth lifted in a slow smile. He draped his forearm over the steering wheel and turned to look at me. "Darned if you don't look good sitting in my truck. Like you belong right there."

My stomach fluttered. Warmth spread through my limbs. I knew the temperatures were below freezing, but right now, I could have melted butter with the touch of my hand. "I spent enough time here—there's probably an indent where I used to sit."

With his arm still draped over the steering wheel, he shook his head, as if he couldn't believe it was me. "I didn't think it was possible."

"What's that? Me coming home?" Hadn't we already covered that?

"No, that you grew prettier since the last time I saw you. How do you do that?"

"I was thinking the same thing about you."

"I do have a pretty face," Jack said, laughing. "Everyone says so."

That was the truth. "All the girls in high school were in love with you."

"Nah, I'm too ornery and wild for most of the women in this town. You were the only one who could ever put up with me for long."

"That's not true." What about Helen? I was itching to ask but decided to wait. I didn't want to be that obvious. Not when I'd only just gotten home. A girl should be subtle in matters of the heart.

The moment was over too soon. Turning toward the front window, Jack put the truck in gear and pulled out of the lot. Soon, we were headed down the country road toward town. "Fresh snow?" I asked.

"Last night. First big one of the season. Just for you."

I warmed again. Was he flirting with me? I never knew these things. At college, the girls had teased me that I never knew when a man was interested in me. Not that I cared. I didn't want any of those soft, weak young men. No one could compare to Jack. "How are your folks?"

"Over the moon. Henry and Lillian had a baby. A boy—named Jack after me. They call him Jay, though."

"My mother told me about the baby." Everyone was married and having babies. All but me. I should keep it that way if I wanted to have a career in the family business. The minute I had a baby or even a husband, everyone would expect me to stay home and behave myself.

"I never thought Henry would settle down without so much as a fight," Jack said, sounding slightly disgusted. "That woman owns his soul."

"God forbid one of the Depaul men is tamed." Both the Depaul boys had been sweet as ice cream, but Henry was more playful and carefree. Jack had always had an intensity about him. One he channeled into his father's farm. Or, at least, that was his plan back when we were in high school. He'd been a good student but had no interest in going to college. "My place is here," he'd said to me on our graduation night. "With my family and our horses."

"Yeah, you'd hardly recognize him. Enamored with his wife and baby—everything is about them. As it should be, of course. But it's still a little strange for me. Everything changes, I guess."

11

"I know all about that—my siblings have all fallen, one by one, until there's only one left."

"You want it that way forever?" He glanced over at me and raised an eyebrow. "Are you still determined to conquer the world?"

"I'm not sure. The world wasn't quite how I thought it would be."

"The world's loss is my gain—I mean *our* gain. The town collectively."

My chest warmed. He'd missed me. "I don't want a man telling me what to do. I know that."

He shook his head, chuckling. "I pity the man who tries." He turned off the main highway to the road out to my parents' estate.

I drank in the beauty of the frozen, leafless branches of the aspens. I'd missed them. And the fields and the smell of woodsmoke in the air. "I've missed home more than you can imagine."

"Not having left, I can't really."

"What about you and Helen?" I asked, wanting to know and not wanting to at the same time. "Are you getting married soon?"

"Helen, no." His voice thickened. "She moved back home six months ago."

"She did?" I sat up straighter just as we bounced through a pothole in the road. My teeth clanked together. I held on to the seat with both hands tucked under my legs. Why hadn't any of my sisters told me that? It was a deliberate omission, I felt sure. They were up to something.

"Yeah, she broke it off—said I loved my horses more than her. It was all very dramatic."

I sucked in my cheeks to keep from smiling. He was free. Or was there someone else? A man like Jack Depaul didn't stay unattached for long. "You have another girl, then?"

"Nah. I decided after Helen, I'd rather wait."

"For what?" I peered at him, taking in the strength of his profile with that square jaw and high cheekbones.

He turned slowly toward me. "For you to come home. There's no one else who can compete with you, Miss Barnes. There never was and never will be. Helen had it wrong. It's not the horses I put ahead of her, it was you."

2

JACK

Had I said it? Yes, I'd said the words I'd kept to myself for years and years. Delphia Barnes. Here she was in my truck, blushing like the pink hydrangeas in my mother's garden. I'd never seen her look more attractive, and that was saying something. God had made her about as perfect as a woman could be, pretty inside and out.

She stared at me, her full mouth slightly open, before she shifted slightly and smoothed the collar of her coat, which had been perfectly flat to begin with.

I stole another glance at her. She wore an overcoat in a lighter shade of blue, with two buttons displayed at the tuck of the waist. A dark blue derby hat with a white feather was fastened at the back of her head. Her fair hair, the color of late-summer grasses, was carefully arranged in large curls that bobbed at her shoulders. She'd cut it when we were in high school, as most of the girls had back then. Their transformation from little girls with pigtails and bowler hats to curvy young women had seemed to happen overnight. Either that, or we were too knuckleheaded to notice. Until we suddenly did. Girls

14

whom we had disliked and stayed far away from were suddenly interesting.

Then, a kind of panicked expression overtook her even features. I'd embarrassed her. Obviously. She looked away, gazing out the side window.

I darted a look at her feet. A pair of high-heeled shoes were clasped at her ankle, showing off the shapely swell of her calves.

Finally, she seemed to compose herself enough to look at me. "Jack Depaul, are you flirting with me?" She said it lightly, but her eyes told me a different story. I'd surprised her and perhaps intrigued her. Had she not known how smitten with her I'd always been? At the moment, it appeared she'd had nary a clue. Did she have any of the same feelings? If not, I'd just made a complete fool of myself.

I almost opened my big mouth to tell her that I had more than a few women interested in me. After Helen and I decided against marrying, they'd come out of the shadows. I'd be walking downtown and one or two would suddenly appear, as if they'd only happened upon me, when I had a feeling they knew my routines and had timed the chance encounter perfectly. But I kept that to myself. My mother hated a braggart. She said if something were true, it was evident without having to bring it to anyone's attention. So I kept quiet. The last thing I wanted was for Delphia to think I'd gotten too big for my britches since she'd been away.

"Tell me more about Helen."

Helen? Why was she asking me about Helen? What did she have to do with anything? She never really had, which had been the trouble. I'd hoped she would become as important to me as Delphia. I'd tried. I really had. "What do you want to know?"

"Were you in love with her?"

Hadn't I just admitted the contrary? She could never hold up against the memory of Delphia. I'd finally decided to give in and admit to myself that I couldn't fall in love with Helen. Not when I loved Delphia. "Um, no. I was not in love with her."

"Then why did you date her so long? My mother told me she thought you would get engaged. All I heard when I asked about you was about this beautiful young woman who had moved to town."

Helen had moved with her family to Emerson Pass after Delphia left for college. She'd become good friends with Lillian, my brother's wife. We'd fallen into a pattern of double dating. I'd hoped to grow to love Helen, and maybe I would have if my heart hadn't belonged to someone else.

"We dated long enough for both of us to know it wasn't right between us. After the big scene, where she demanded to know if I planned on marrying her, she left for Georgia. She wrote to me a few months later to tell me she'd married a young man she'd known all her life. Someone much more appropriate for her kind." I chuckled. "She added that last part to hurt me a little."

"Did it?"

"Nah. I didn't have strong enough feelings for it to hurt. Do you know what I mean?"

"Sure I do." She blinked, then looked down at her lap. "And you don't miss her?"

"Honestly, no. She's a perfectly fine person, but we weren't suited. She hated it here, for one thing. Anyway, I'm happy for her. She's content now." I didn't mention how *discontent* she'd been here and how vocal she'd been about it: the nights were too cold, the air too dry, the scent of woodsmoke made her eyes water, the town was too quiet. Her list of complaints went on and on until one day I asked her why she didn't just return to Georgia. She'd looked at me as if the idea had never occurred to her. A few weeks later, she was gone.

"How nice for her to know where she belonged," Delphia

said in a dry, ironic tone. "But how could she hate it here? That makes no sense whatsoever."

Why were we still talking about Helen? Clearly, Delphia was curious about her. Had she been wondering all along about Helen and me? Was she jealous? *God, please let it be so,* I silently prayed. "Said it was too cold."

"People say that," Delphia said. "When they don't understand that all you need is another layer of clothes and all is well."

"My horses scared her, too."

Her blue eyes snapped with impatience. "Well, that won't do. Not for you."

The Barneses' driveway was a half mile up the road. I gripped the steering wheel. I needed to say what had been in my heart for so long. It was time. Who knew what tomorrow would bring? The news of war, surely? Decisions I would have to make. Impending departure, perhaps? I'd waited too long to tell her how I felt. She was home. I had her alone. We were both free. Now was the time.

I knew the minute we arrived at her parents' place, she would be mobbed by family members. "I'm going to pull off here so we can talk for a moment."

She raised one eyebrow and nodded.

I veered off the road into a spot often used to turn around and go the other direction and shut off the engine. The afternoon was quiet, without the sound of birds or other critters because of the time of year and deep snowfall. Although it was cold, I loved this season. It was as if God gave us a little reprieve from the noises of everyday life for a few months. The world became only a whisper, leaving room to think and breathe.

"Why all the questions about Helen?" I asked, shifting to get a better look at her.

She lifted her pointy chin and shrugged, gazing out the front window. "I wanted to know about the woman you were fixed to marry. She occupied too many of my thoughts, if you want to know the truth."

"Why's that?"

"Don't be dense," she said.

I laughed, delighted that she was admitting to being jealous. If she'd only known that my thoughts always returned immediately to her, she needn't have worried. "We were never engaged. People just assumed we were because we were often together at events and such." It sounded lame to say out loud, but it was true. Rumors started after I took her out a few times. People assumed we would get engaged. "Helen's mother helped that rumor along."

"Can't blame her for that. She knew you were the finest man in town."

That took my breath away. "Do you think that? Truly?"

She shifted in the seat to turn my direction, pressing her knees together. "I've always known that to be true. Who else in this world is like you? No one. Wasn't that obvious at graduation night?"

I warmed at the memory. Her mouth had been warm and inviting. I'd have liked to kiss her all night. However, I'd been so surprised, and a little tipsy from the spiked punch, that I'd stood there like an idiot. "You said it was the punch," I said.

"*You* said it was the punch."

"The truth is, I didn't want to hold you back. My feelings for you were real, but I wasn't sure yours were. If I'd have held you back in any way, I would never have forgiven myself. You were like a wild horse back then. You needed to run free. If you came home eventually and still wanted me, then I would know it was right. But not before you were allowed to run."

"I'm not sure I understand," Delphia said. "Say it plainly."

"If I'd told you how much I cared about you, I was worried you'd feel obligated to make a choice. I didn't want you to have to choose between college and me. That's not the way to love a woman, holding her so tightly she can't breathe."

"Who says that would have even been a possibility?" She lifted that chin of hers again. "You think a lot of yourself."

I laughed. "Your kiss said a whole lot of things you hadn't said before." I kept my voice light, even though my words were the absolute truth. "Wasn't something I soon forgot, I can tell you that."

"What are you saying, Jack? That you've carried a torch for me all these years?"

"Is that hard to believe?" I took her in, the creaminess of her complexion, the way she sucked her cheeks inward when she was thinking. "It was the light of a thousand torches, if you want to know the truth."

"It's a little hard to believe. Not because I'm not great, of course." She gave me a cheeky grin. "But because you could have your pick of women in this town or anywhere else, for that matter."

True. But again, no one liked a braggart.

"What's that have to do with my feelings for you?" I asked, reaching across the seat of my truck to brush away a clump of hair that had stuck to her cheek. "No one is you." Her skin was damp and warm. Nerves? Excitement? It wasn't the weather. With the engine off, the cab of the truck had turned cold almost immediately. I was glad she wore a pair of leather gloves so her hands wouldn't get cold as we sat here.

"That's why you haven't said anything before now." She seemed to be taking this in, her gaze directed out the front window.

I hesitated, wanting to say this the right way. "I wouldn't have been able to forgive myself if I stood in the way of your dreams."

"You think I would have stayed home had I known you cared

for me that way?" She peered at me with humor dancing in her blue eyes.

I grinned and wrapped one of her curls around my finger. "I'm hard to resist."

"You think a lot of yourself." She laughed and reached out to smooth down the collar of my coat, as she'd done to her own moments ago. I could easily envision that hand on my skin instead. "I've been bothered by the idea of this Helen. I'm now adjusting to the idea of her no longer being in the way."

My heart leaped. "In the way of what?" I asked softly.

"You know."

"Do I?"

"I don't know how you haven't," Delphia said. "Ever since the night of our graduation party—the way we'd danced together earlier—the way my heart seemed to beat with a new rhythm."

I could hardly breathe. Finally, after all these years, we were talking about our true feelings. "That's the night I knew for sure. Before that, I'd admired your beauty and cleverness, but you were just my friend. Maybe it was seeing you in that dress or holding you in my arms, but suddenly, I knew."

She looked down at her hands, twisting her fingers together. "The whole evening seemed magical. I've told myself it was only the romance of the night playing tricks on my mind. And the punch. You've never been far from my thoughts." A muscle in her right cheek twitched.

"But? I feel there's more," I said.

"I don't know if I'm the type of girl to settle down and have babies. Even though I'm home, I want to have a career of my own outside of the house. Most men wouldn't care for that idea at all."

"I know you, Delphia. Better than anyone, I bet. I'd never try to change you. I don't want you to be like everyone else. You're special." She'd been at the top of our class without even trying. Especially in our math classes, she'd known the answer long before the rest of us. I'd understood how happy learning new skills made her and how she craved the excitement of using her mind to solve problems. There was no way she would be satisfied with a traditional role as a wife and mother. I'd have never asked her to do so.

"Could you see yourself married to me?" I asked. "If I were to give you the freedom to do what made you happy?"

She took her time answering. Meanwhile, I was a mass of nerves. "I could see that, yes. Very easily, in fact. Being away made me realize how much the people I left behind mean to me. Especially you." She looked into my eyes.

My mouth seemed to be controlled by a happy puppet master, as I couldn't stop smiling. "You'll give me a chance, then?"

"Will you give me a chance?" She lifted her hand as if to touch me but withdrew and let it rest on her lap instead.

"I'll do anything for you," I said. Even let her go, which I'd done. But now? Was there a chance for us to be happy together?

"I'd be lying if I didn't admit how much I've longed to see you and be with you," Delphia said. "I'm sorry it took so long."

"You're worth waiting for."

"Oh, Jack. Thank you."

"Tomorrow, may I take you dancing at the club?" I asked. "The one you will soon run?"

"Yes, that would be fine. Dinner too?"

"Dinner too." The whole world, if she wanted it. Whatever it took, I would make it happen.

She was quiet for a few seconds, tugging at the collar of her coat once again. "If we go to war, will you enlist?"

The question seemed to come out of nowhere and deflated my jubilant mood. War was inevitable. I would not be able to stand aside while others enlisted. "I'll have to. No self-respecting man will be able to shrink away out of cowardice."

"I'm scared. Our lives are going to change if we go to war."

"They will change. But maybe it will be quick. American troops could turn everything around. We can get in and out, and the world can move forward."

She nodded. "Wouldn't that be wonderful?"

"You don't sound convinced."

"I grew up listening to my mother talk about the first war. She said they all thought it would be done quickly. It wasn't." Her eyes glistened. "I don't know how we'll stand to let you all go. The years when my brothers served during the Great War were the worst times of my parents' life."

"This won't be easy. But we'll do it anyway. We have to fight against tyranny."

"Yes, we do. Of course, we do. It's just that—I'm frightened. For you. For our families. Bleu and Beaumont will want to enlist. You know they will."

She was right. The four of us had been such good friends in high school for a reason. We thought the same way about life. Courage and duty were paramount to our belief systems.

"We have to put our trust in God," I said.

We were quiet for a moment. A snowflake hit my windshield.

"Maybe it won't come to that," she said finally. "I've just come home. I don't want to see you all leave."

"Like you, we'll be back."

She shivered, either from worry or cold. Regardless of which, I started the truck and put it into gear.

Delphia put her hand on my arm. "Before we go."

"Yes?" I turned to look at her, both hands on the wheel.

She smiled and tilted her head sideways. "Would you like to kiss me? This time without the aid of the punch?"

"Are you sure? You just got home. I don't want to rush you." I was instantly nervous. I'd dreamt of this moment for too long to mess it up now.

"It's been four and a half years. I think it's about time.

Anyway, are you going to kiss me or talk some more?" Delphia asked.

"I'm going to kiss you." I leaned over the seat and cupped her chin in my gloved hand. How had I never noticed how giant my hands were compared to her face? I was glad for the gloves. My skin was calloused and rough from working outside and with the horses. Her delicate skin deserved better than that.

She drew in a breath and stared up at me. "I've suddenly lost my nerve. I haven't kissed anyone since you."

How was that possible? "Really? I figured you had a ton of beaux at school."

"Not unless you count our old house cat, Toby. He liked to lick my arm while I was studying."

"Toby's a smart cat." I traced a finger down her slender neck. "Here I've been, imagining you kissing all the boys and going to all the dances."

"I went to some dances. But no one ever appealed to me. They all seemed soft compared to the boys from home."

"Boys?"

"All right, you. I don't think any of them could lasso a runaway horse as if it were as easy as breathing."

"It's not that easy." I kept my gaze on her pink mouth.

"Did you kiss Helen a lot?" Delphia asked.

I shrugged one shoulder. "Sure. Some."

"You must have enjoyed it then?"

"Kissing is nice, yes. But she wasn't you."

"So you say." Her eyes flashed, that old competitive streak in her coming to the surface.

"Do you want me to kiss you or not?" I asked, teasing. "Because you have to be quiet for a few seconds."

She clamped her lips together and gave me a facetious smile.

I leaned closer. "Now, no fidgeting, or you'll spook me."

She nodded but didn't say anything further. I took that as my opening and drew closer before placing my mouth on hers. Like

23

I'd said, I'd shared quite a few kisses with Helen, all pleasant but nothing that made my toes tingle. They were tingling now.

As was the rest of me.

Her lips were pliant and soft under mine but also confident, returning my kiss without any hint of shyness. Delphia Barnes! Who would have thought this terrible day in history would be such a grand day for me? She'd come home at last. And maybe, just maybe, she might love me too.

Finally, we parted. "I have to get you home or your mother will worry," I said.

"Yes, I suppose so."

I drove slowly down the driveway, wishing this moment could last forever. Soon, though, we were at the house. Several additional cars were parked out by the barn. Her entire family would be here to welcome her home.

"Would you like to come in?" Delphia asked.

"No, you go. Be with your family. They're all very excited to see you. Your mother mentioned something about a turkey dinner since you missed Thanksgiving."

Her eyes shone in the dim light. Snow was falling more heavily now. I had only a short way to drive to my family's farm, so I wasn't worried. Still, I knew it was time to let her go. For now, anyway.

"I'll see you tomorrow," she said.

"Yes. Let me walk you to the door."

I went around to help her down from the truck. The driveway had been plowed, leaving it muddy. She looked down at the ground. "My good shoes will be ruined."

"Not to worry, my dear," I said. "I shall carry you to the door." Before she could protest, I scooped her out of my truck. She weighed less than a few hay bales. I grabbed her suitcase from the back with my free hand. She wrapped both her arms around my neck. In no time at all, I had her delivered to the front door. We hesitated for a moment under the awning of the front porch, staring into each other's eyes. Then I tore my gaze from her and let it rest briefly on the windows of the Barneses' sitting room. Her family would be waiting there for her.

Reluctantly, I set her and her case down on the porch. Under the light from the porch lamp, her eyes appeared even bluer than before. They peeked up at me from her delicate face, portraying a hint of surprise and shyness. I'd managed to take her aback. I'm not sure in the years of our friendship I'd ever done so. She was off-kilter and yet didn't seem to mind. "I'll pick you up at seven tomorrow," I said. "Regardless of the state of the world, I'd like to dance with you as if the night will never end."

"You've grown sentimental on me," she said huskily.

"You were gone a long time, allowing me time to see with clarity what was before me all along."

Her gaze drifted past me to the yard. Snow fell heavily now. "There's nothing as pretty as Colorado snow, is there?"

"I'd disagree." Even Colorado couldn't compare to the woman in front of me.

"I'll be ready at seven." She smiled, dazzling me with her beauty, before turning away to go inside.

I stood on the porch for a few seconds, listening to her call out, "Family, I'm home."

Then, more voices and footsteps. I sprinted down the stairs and out to my truck. What did the future hold for America? What did it hold for me?

All I knew at the moment? The girl I loved might possibly love me too. That was good enough for now.

THAT EVENING, my family gathered as we always did for Sunday supper. My brother Henry and Lillian were already in the kitchen with my mother when Papa and I came in from our last chores of the day. Baby Jay sat in the old wooden high chair that had once been Henry's and then mine, pounding his fists into the tray and babbling happily.

"Howdy, folks," I said before kissing my nephew's sweet head. "Everyone all right?" I knew the answer. My mother's face was pallid and her mouth pinched. Lillian's was about the same. Henry, normally quiet, seemed to have drawn even more inside himself.

Papa and I exchanged a look. It would be up to us to boost everyone's mood tonight. "Papa, should we have a bottle of wine tonight?"

"A French Bordeaux, do you think? Maybe some dancing?" Papa grabbed Mama by her slender waist and twirled her around the kitchen.

Our home had been built on the property Lord Barnes had gifted my parents for their dedicated service to his family a few years before Henry was born. Papa's passion had been and remained horses. He and my mother set out to breed fine horses and sell them for a good profit. They'd done well. Our log home might be rustic looking on the outside, but my mother had decorated it beautifully with thick rugs, attractive light fixtures, and plush yet comfortable furniture. We spent a great deal of time as a family in the kitchen. Our cook and housekeeper, Georgina, was off on Sundays, so my mother and Lillian always worked together to prepare our family meal. I looked forward to these evenings all week.

Tonight, however, we were not a jovial bunch. It was impossible not to think about what had happened in Hawaii. While Papa, Henry, and I tended to the chores, my mother and Lillian had sat by the radio. Reports of more deaths came in every hour. I was sick, thinking about those poor young navy men perishing from Japanese bombs. They'd probably gotten up that morning and done whatever their duties were and then maybe had breakfast. Only to be killed an hour later.

We all sat down in the dining room to eat at about half past six. The ladies had prepared a pork roast with potatoes, onions, and carrots. It was delicious, but none of us had much of an appetite. I forced it down, making several comments about how good it was. Papa seemed to be trying his best to keep our minds off the frightening news of the day by talking about the talents of our latest foal. She'd come at midnight the night before. The two of us had been with the mother for most of the labor. My aunt Poppy was a veterinarian and would have come if we needed her, but there was no need. Papa and I had helped a lot of colts into this world. Unless there was a complication, we didn't need her.

Last night was about as smooth a birth as we'd ever had. Ironic, I thought, when the Japanese were headed across the sea to kill innocent Americans. It was hard to understand how something as precious and delightful as the birth of a perfect baby filly could happen in the same world as evil dictators.

None of us wanted to bring up the subject of enlistment, but I knew it was heavy on all our minds. My mother would be thinking only of her sons. Papa, too, for that matter. He and his family had come over from France when he was a teenager. His little sister, Poppy, had been a child. When their parents died, he'd lucked into a job with Lord Barnes, caring for his animals and the gardens. My mother had worked in the house as a maid. When they fell in love and married, Lord Barnes gifted them with a wooded piece of property. They'd taken that gift and made it into the business that it was today. We were known throughout several states to be the best horse breeders around. My brother and I had been born into the business but loved it as if we'd chosen it ourselves. Horses ran through our blood as much as the ground on which we walked every day. Neither of us had ever wished for anything other than to continue to build on the work of our parents. Until now. If we went to war, Henry and I would have to go.

27

My father had been following the events overseas carefully. Although he hadn't been to France since he emigrated, it was his heritage. What happened there was of great concern to him. This was yet another reason my brother and I would have to go.

Jay started to fuss in his high chair. Lillian sighed and got up to get him. "No, let me," I said. "You eat while it's still hot."

Lillian tapped her mouth with one of my mother's carefully ironed cloth napkins. "Are you sure?"

I was already up and grabbing Jay from his high chair. He kicked his fat legs against my chest and babbled happily. Or at least it seemed that way to me. I held him with one arm and bounced him on my knee. At a little over a year old, he was walking and getting into all kinds of trouble. Lillian said he didn't stop moving from the moment he woke until the moment he passed out from exhaustion. He had Henry's dark hair but Lillian's light green eyes with thick lashes.

"Jay, do you want some of my potato?" I asked him.

He buried a chubby pink cheek into my chest and shook his head.

"He's contrary lately," Henry said absently.

"My husband thinks this is a good thing." Lillian sent an indulgent smile over to my brother.

"His uncle Jack was the same way," Mother said. "Why walk when he could run?"

I let my gaze linger on my pretty mother. With her smooth skin, she looked too young to be the mother of two grown men. She'd always worn her sun hat, she said when people asked her how she kept her youthful appearance. Just a touch of silver had infused her honey-colored locks. When I'd been young, she'd worn her long hair pulled back in a bun, but these days it was cut to fall at her shoulders in a sleek bob.

All my life, she'd been quiet and steady, like Henry. I'd never seen her come undone, even during times of stress. A war in which her sons had to enlist, though? That would be the one thing that would challenge her calm demeanor.

"What is it, Jack?" Papa asked. "You look a million miles away."

I blinked and turned my attention to my father. His brown eyes always made me feel as if a warm blanket were wrapped around my shoulders. He was strong as any of our Thoroughbred horses and worked harder than any man I'd ever known. As a child, I didn't think there was anything he couldn't do. Now, I knew his limitations, seeing him as a man instead of my father. Still, I admired him for his work ethic, his integrity and fairness when it came to business, and the way he took care of our mother.

We were a happy family. Simple, maybe, but content. I'd never thought that would ever change. But war threatened everything, including us.

3

DELPHIA

Before dinner on that first evening I was home, my father asked Phillip, Flynn, and me to join him in his study. He poured us all a whiskey, me included, which surprised me. Was it possible they could see me as an equal member of our family team? None of the other women in our family had ever shown interest in being part of any aspect of our business. My father had continued to buy land and buildings in Colorado and Illinois, namely Chicago, most of which he leased out to others, bringing in much more than he'd spent. There was the ski mountain, which Flynn and Phillip ran, as well as the lodge. The nightclub had always been part of the resort, but when I'd been home last, they'd expressed fatigue over the day-to-day running of it. Now that liquor was legal again, everything was much less risky. Raids by the police could no longer happen, and there was no fear of jail time. The sheriff had looked the other way back then, but things were different in the modern era. More scrutiny had become necessary as our town grew. Even Papa, who had enjoyed running things the way he wanted, had accepted that he could no longer influence the authorities as he once had. It was one thing when we were a burgeoning frontier town. Quite another now that we were a community of several thousand. The law had become more important to keep our citizens safe.

Papa gestured for me to take the leather chair in front of the fire. My mother's chair. She and Papa sat together many nights reading or talking in here. The sitting room was large and harder to heat. Now that their nest was almost empty, they only used it when the family got together.

I settled into the spot on the cushion where my mother's small frame had made a permanent indentation. It fit me perfectly. I was slender like my mother, with her same narrow hips and flat chest. Not a curve to be found. My sisters, other than Addie, had a little more girth to them, probably from their real mother. Addie and I had taken after our mother in many ways, including our fair hair and skin, but not her big brown eyes. Mine were a medium blue, and Addie's a few shades lighter than that.

"Shannon's put her foot down about the club," Flynn said. "She hates it, you know, for obvious reasons, and wants me out of it completely."

I nodded. He referred to an incident in the twenties when he'd had the bright idea to make and distribute moonshine to his club as well as others. Unfortunately, his little side business had caught the attention of some mobsters from Chicago, who subsequently threatened our family and the idyllic way of life for the residents of Emerson Pass. All had ended well, thankfully. My family, mostly Cymbeline and her pistol, had convinced the dangerous men to leave us alone. However, the aftermath, including destroying the distillery, had caused everyone involved a lot of angst. Flynn had almost lost his wife and family over his desire to build an empire separate from the one my father had already built. I understood this need to have something of your own, but it had been the wrong choice for everyone. Although we would never abandon one of our own, my parents were not pleased. It had taken some doing on his part, but Flynn had eventually redeemed himself. Since then, he and Shannon had lived in harmony, raising their two little girls. My sister-in-law was sweet but strong. One would have to be to be married to my brother.

"Jo has expressed a similar sentiment," Phillip said before taking a sip of his drink. His dark hair had become salt-and-pepper since I'd been at school. It suited him. He was now distinguished in addition to being strikingly handsome with that strong jawline and intense blue eyes. "Even though we're not supposed to have to be there at night, it seems inevitable that Scotty calls us at least once a week."

"Scotty?" I asked.

"Our new manager," Flynn said. He flicked a stray curl from his forehead. Strangely enough, neither he nor his twin, my brother Theo, had any white or silver in their brown hair. Their faces had thinned a little now that they were forty, but not much else gave away their age. "He's hopeless."

"And hapless," Phillip said. "Poor man."

"He can't tie his shoes without calling one of us," Flynn said. "We need you to fire him right away."

"Me? Why can't one of you fire him?" I asked, alarmed. I'd not thought about having to fire someone. It seemed rather unpleasant and potentially messy. Especially in this town where everyone knew everyone else's business.

"We've tried," Phillip said, sighing. "Truly, we have."

"But somehow, we end up keeping him." Flynn raised his glass toward the fireplace, where freshly stoked logs warmed the room. "He's got this way of distracting a fellow until it's too late."

"By the time we come to, so to speak, he's already left the room," Phillip said. "And on to his next task that he makes a mess of."

"As in?" I asked. "Give me an example of this hapless Scotty."

"He can't balance the books, for one," Phillip said, rolling his eyes. "Every month I have to go back in and redo it all."

"The staff dislikes him immensely." Flynn placed two fingers above his right eyebrow as if the very thought of this Scotty gave him a headache. "His greatest gift seems to be getting the staff to do his job and then taking credit for it."

"Terrible," Papa murmured. "I despise that in a leader."

"He's not a leader, that's the trouble," Flynn said.

"Last week he ordered twice as much whiskey as we needed but left gin off the order completely." Phillip grimaced. "We had some unhappy customers for a week. You know how the women are about their gin and tonics."

I didn't know but figured I would soon enough.

"One time he actually had us agreeing to a raise. It's the darnedest thing." Flynn emptied his glass and rose from the hardback chair nearest the fire to fill his drink.

"We can't explain it," Phillip said. "But we're embarrassed. If it weren't that it's happened to both of us on separate occasions, I'd think it was something wrong with me."

"No, it can't be," Flynn said. "We're good at our jobs. Usually, anyway."

"We need you to give him some sass and fire his sorry behind," Flynn said.

I glanced at Papa, who was staring into the fire with an amused lift to his mouth. His eyes always seemed as if they were laughing of their own accord. My mother often said she thought he was amused by her when they first met. To which my father had said, "I was too busy worshipping you to laugh at you."

"Sis, you can do it," Flynn said.

"Either that or we're going to have to put Cym on the job," Phillip said.

"We don't want to ruin the man's life." Flynn moved to stand by the fire, warming his backside. "But we really need him gone."

My father nodded thoughtfully. "It's the perfect time to ease him out gracefully. Your sister's come home and wants to run the club."

"And we want to keep it in the family whenever possible," Flynn said. "Makes perfect sense."

"Until you're face-to-face with the clown," Phillip said. "And then you won't know which end is up."

I smiled to myself. This would be no problem, I told myself. I despised incompetency. There was no reason to keep him. I was an educated woman. Surely I could get rid of him easily.

"All right, I'll do my best," I said. "Maybe I'll have better luck. Fresh eyes, so to speak."

"Great." Flynn grinned. "I haven't felt this free in years. Delphia, welcome home." He raised his glass, and I did the same.

It felt right to be home. I'd hoped it would. After being away for so long, I'd worried about feeling out of place. Sitting here with my family, however, I knew with certainty this was where I belonged.

AFTER DINNER, Papa made all of the grandchildren line up in a row from oldest to youngest so he could take a photograph. He'd recently bought a camera and couldn't stop taking pictures. Mama told me he was making a nuisance of himself, but he didn't care.

I drank them all in, amazed as always that the little ones had changed so much in the year since I'd last been home. Sitting with Addie on the big chair we used to share as children, contentment made me warm and drowsy. I'd had my adventures and tamed my rebellious spirit. Now I could do interesting work, perhaps even take some of the burdens of the business from Flynn and Phillip.

Flynn and Theo, along with their wives and family, excused

themselves after the photographing was finished. Louisa, Theo's wife, had given me a tight hug and apologized for leaving early. There was a baby coming out at the Murphys'. She and Theo were headed there after dropping the nanny and their children off at home.

Addie's husband, James, was with Papa and the rest of the men in the formal parlor on the other end of the house. The women had retired to the sitting room. I looked around the room, happy to be in the company of my sisters. Josephine, slim and regal, wore a dark blue dinner dress and a string of pearls. She'd not aged much since I'd been gone. Her daughters and her work at the library kept her engaged and inspired. Poppy and Quinn, my nieces, were now in their early twenties. Poppy, the older of the two, had become a librarian and now worked at the library her mother had started. Quinn was in her last year at university in Chicago, studying to be a teacher like the woman she was named after. There was a symmetry to it all that pleased Jo. She'd been a wonderful mother. If I'd thought I could do as well as she had, I might consider becoming one myself. If I were with Jack—well, never mind about that. I must not get ahead of myself.

Fiona looked lovely, if not a little shattered by the news of the day. She had on a pale pink dress and a string of sparkly sapphires around her neck. After adopting Bleu and Beaumont, my sister and Li had had three more children. Ironically, another set of twin boys, named James and Alexander, and then a little girl named Cassandra, whom everyone called Cassie.

Cymbeline, wearing a black sleeveless cocktail dress that showed off her muscular arms, poured herself a sherry and then plopped onto the love seat next to Fiona. She discarded her shoes and rubbed the arch of one of them with her thumb. "My feet ache. Viktor has me training for an exhibition in January. Ridiculous, really. It's not like I can really compete anymore. I'm as old as the hills."

35

Mama, who had her knitting in her lap, looked up from unraveling a ball of red yarn. "Darling, you're hardly old."

"For a ski jumper, I am," Cym said. "Thank goodness you all talked me into having children, or I'd be utterly useless and bored."

"Come, give me those feet," Fiona said to Cym.

Cym grinned and scooted to the far end of the couch, then stuck her feet, covered in silk stockings, onto Fiona's lap. "I missed you while you were in California."

"I missed you all as well," Fiona said. "I'm not sure we'll go away again, even for such good work. It's too hard on our family."

"Did the children stay with Mama while you and Li were away?" I asked Fiona.

She nodded. "For an entire month. Bleu and Beaumont could have looked after them, but they're busy with their jobs now. And Mama likes to have them here with her while we're gone. We couldn't have made the trip without her. It was a great opportunity and lucrative, but I missed the kids."

"They do just fine without you," Mama said. "But they're always happy when you return."

I snuggled closer to Addie. She wore a red dress that complemented her fair skin and hair. There wasn't much to her, but she was warm and felt so familiar. I put my head on her shoulder. "Did you miss me as much as I missed you?"

"More so," Addie said.

"She's been busy becoming famous and everything," Fiona said, teasing. "I'm surprised she has time for us."

Addie smiled and ducked her chin, shy to be the center of attention. "I'd never be too busy for my sisters."

"I'm glad the children weren't at the big table for dinner," I said. "I'm afraid talk of war would scare them."

"I agree." Fiona nodded at Josephine, who was at the bar pouring sherry. I declined. Sherry was not for me. A good gin and tonic, yes. However, Mama didn't like it when we had cocktails she thought should be reserved only for men, so I abstained. So many changes had happened since the time she was my age. A world war, the Depression, the end of Prohibition, more women going to college than ever before. And now, another war.

At dinner, with the little children eating downstairs with several of my sisters' nannies, we'd been able to speak about the events of the day. Papa felt sure the news would come tomorrow that we'd declared war on Japan.

Mama had been quiet, as had my sister Fiona. They, in particular, were worried, not just for the state of the world but for the young men we held dear. As I sat listening to the men talk, I thought about what it would mean to my family. We would have to watch Bleu and Beaumont leave us to fight a war across the ocean. Why, why, why? What a waste of life this war was, all because of Hitler.

Bleu and Beaumont had gone to college together in Boulder when I left for the east. Bleu had studied business. Beaumont had studied engineering and architecture. They'd planned on going into business together, building structures and homes, and had already built up a thriving enterprise. Much of the work had been on the buildings Papa owned downtown, equipping them with modern plumbing and electricity.

The three of us had been fast friends, especially in high school. Along with Jack, we'd done a lot together. Days at the river, evenings around a bonfire, studying for exams. Because of the age difference, I was closer to them than I was to my own brothers. Could I bear to see them go as well as Jack? It would be just me left.

"It's hard for me to understand how we're back here again," Mama said without looking up from her knitting. "We already sent one generation off to fight, and now we're back twenty years later to do it all over again? When will it ever be enough?

How many sons and husbands and fathers have to die before the men of this world come to their senses?" She swiped at tears that had gathered at the corners of her eyes and spilled over her cheeks.

Mama was not one to cry. In fact, she was quite stoic most of the time, which couldn't have been easy with all of her children and grandchildren to worry about. Jo crossed the room to sit with Mama. "It will be all right," Jo said.

"The twins will go," Fiona said, voice shaking. "I won't be able to stop them."

"Just as I couldn't when Flynn and Theo enlisted." Mama brought her square of knitting to her cheeks as if it were her handkerchief. "I don't know if I can bear it again. The entire time they were gone, I could barely breathe."

Fiona nodded. "I remember. We were women waiting for word. I guess we'll do it again."

"We'll pray, just as we did then," Mama said. "That our boys will return to us in one piece."

"What did Jack say about it when he picked you up?" Addie asked softly. "He'll want to go too, I suppose?"

"How could he not? All three of them—they won't be able to live with themselves if they don't. They'll see it as cowardice."

"If only they saw it the way we do," Mama said.

"There will be a draft, Mama," Jo said. "They might not be able to avoid it, even if they decided not to enlist."

"Thank God we have so many girls." Cym tilted her face to the ceiling, the back of her head on the arm of the sofa.

"Amen to that," Jo said.

"Fiona, we'll be here for you every moment," Addie said.

Fiona brushed her cheeks. "I know you will. You're all such a comfort to me." Her gaze drifted away from Cym's feet toward the window. "When I think what we saved the boys from, only to send them back there. It's too much." She bit her lip, obviously to keep from crying. But it didn't matter. She would feel it anyway, whether the tears came or not.

"I wish I could fight the lousy bastards," Cym said.

"I do too," I said. Sadly, there wasn't much either of us could do. The world was run by men, while the women were left to weep for their boys.

4

JACK

On the eighth of December, with my brother and Lillian, my parents and I sat around the radio in my parents' sitting room. Dinner waited on the table, but none of us could eat. Instead, we sat in silence as Roosevelt, in front of a cheering crowd of politicians, declared war on Japan.

His sure voice, with the fat consonants of his New England accent, roused my patriotic spirit. Certain phrases caught my attention more than others.

Severe damage...lives lost...torpedoed on the high seas...all measures be taken for our defense...how long it may take us...will win through to absolute victory...unbounding determination...so help us God.

When the speech was over, my father got up from his favorite chair by the fireplace and switched off the radio. No one said anything for a moment. Jay, playing on the floor with his toy truck made of wood, cried out in glee as he rammed it into the side of the sofa. Lillian rushed to him and picked him up, moving him into the middle of the room where he was not as likely to harm my mother's furniture.

"We need a pen for him," Henry said, obviously trying to lighten the mood.

I played with the fringe on a sofa pillow, looking up when I heard my mother sniff. She had one of Papa's handkerchiefs pressed to her mouth.

"Mam, it'll be all right," Henry said. "We'll be in and out of there and home by this time next year."

"So you'll go without any discussion?" Lillian asked Henry more sharply than I'd ever heard her. She was a quiet, gentle woman who adored my brother and their son. "What about us?"

"Without freedom, what do we have then?" Henry asked. "Hitler could come for us too, you know. If we allow them to take all of Europe, then what? We can't sit around waiting for that to happen. Whatever it takes, we must do."

Lillian turned away and scooped up her son, who flailed his chubby legs in protest. She held him tightly against her chest until he successfully wriggled out of her arms and back to his truck, which had somehow disappeared under a chair. I got up to fetch it for him. He squealed and lunged for it, falling down but getting right back up again.

"He's right, dear," Mama said to Lillian. "I don't like it, but it's true that our very way of life is threatened. These men—this Hirohito and Hitler—they're madmen who want to rule the entire world." She started to cry.

My father pulled her to him and kissed the top of her head. "We have to be brave," he whispered.

"I'm not brave," Mama said. "I don't want to send my boys, my babies, off to war."

"Mama, we're tough," I said. "Country boys. Horsemen. We'll be fine."

She lifted her gaze to mine, eyes glassy with tears. "How I hope that's true."

Henry stood and went to stand before the fire. "Will we go together, brother? To enlist?"

41

I nodded, knowing it was what must be done. I thought of Delphia. Finally home, and now I would have to go. As my father said, we must be brave. "Trust in God, Mama. He'll be with us."

"Yes, God will be with us," Henry said. "Just like you taught us."

I glanced at my watch. It was nearing the time I needed to leave to pick Delphia up for our date. How many would we get before I left? "I have to go. I don't want to make Delphia wait."

My mother nodded, a slight smile lifting the corners of her mouth. "My son taking out Lord Barnes's daughter. What a thing."

"What do you mean?" Lillian asked. She hadn't grown up in Emerson Pass as Henry and I had, thus didn't fully understand the respect and admiration most of us felt toward Alexander Barnes. He was the informal leader of our little spot in the world. The whole town looked to him for guidance. Even with all the success my father and mother have had with their business, they never forgot that it was Delphia's father who had so generously gifted them land and a loan to get them started with their first horses.

"I can remember the day Quinn arrived like it was yesterday," Mama said. "She was so lovely, although skinny as a rail. Lizzie had to put some meat on her bones. What a woman she was—well-educated even though her family was as poor as church mice. She had to come out here so her sister and mother wouldn't starve to death out in Boston. Have I ever told you the first time I met her? She wouldn't let me dress her—said she wasn't used to such things and would be fine on her own. Lizzie and I couldn't believe such an angel had come to us. She saved them all, and us too. Did you know she encouraged me to tell your father how I felt about him?"

"We were besotted with each other, but neither of us knew,"

Papa said, smiling at the memory. Even though I'd heard the story before, I never tired of it.

"And then we married and Quinn treated me as an equal to her," Mama said. "We had such fun—raising all of you youngsters up together."

"You *were* her equal," Lillian said. "Why would you think otherwise?"

"I was a maid in their home," Mama said with a hint of disapproval in her voice. She loved Lillian, but sometimes my sister-in-law's lack of respect when it came to the ways of Emerson Pass frustrated her. Lillian was of the new world, one where class structure meant little. Having grown up in an upper-class home in Denver with maids of her own, it never occurred to Lillian that she should be anything else but privileged. I didn't blame her for it. But my parents were from another time and place. They were immigrants without much but the clothes on their backs when they came to this country. Much of what they had today had been because of their hard work in combination with the generosity of Alexander Barnes. "Timid and without many skills, I was," Mama said, continuing. "But they gave me work just the same. I was grateful for it then and remain so to this day."

"We've told you what Lord Barnes did for us?" Papa asked Lillian.

"Many times," Lillian said drily. We were all on edge tonight, our usual politeness frayed somewhat, I thought. Otherwise, she would realize how rude she was being.

My mother swept her hand around the room. "All of this is because of him. We were nothing more than a housemaid and groundskeeper—young and inexperienced and without a penny to our name. He treated us as equals when he didn't have to. Quinn, too. We won't ever forget it, and I hope you kids won't either."

Lillian flushed and looked down at her lap. Her lips trembled as if trying to keep from bursting into tears. All of it was too much, I thought. My mother shouldn't scold Lillian. Not tonight when we were all afraid.

"We know, Mama," Henry said. "But that was a long time ago. You're no longer a maid."

"It's important we remain humble," Papa said. "No matter what good fortune has come our way."

"We understand," I said, hoping to avoid an argument. "Don't we, Henry? Lillian?"

"Sometimes I wonder if we all forget that *Lord* Barnes is a man, not God," Henry said.

I'd never heard my brother say anything of the sort. I stared at him, shocked at the bitterness that had crept into his tone. I felt a rush of indignation for the father of the woman I loved. Anyway, why were we arguing about any of this? The real enemy here was Japan and Germany. Not one another.

"Lord Barnes is a great man," Papa said. "It's best you remember that."

"Yes, sir." Henry's tone belied his respectful words.

"Henry, come on now." I must keep my temper from flaring and making everything worse. However, my brother angered me. "This is silly. We love the Barnes family and owe them a lot. That's all they're saying."

"If I had a nickel," Lillian said under her breath, but loud enough we all heard her.

My mother visibly flinched. Papa patted Mama's hand before getting up to help himself to a whiskey from the decanter we kept filled but rarely drank from. In fact, Papa kept it for when Lord Barnes or any of Delphia's brothers or brothers-in-law visited for their monthly poker game.

I rose to my feet, hoping to steer this in a different direction. "What do you think of my new suit? Mr. Olofsson did a remarkable job, don't you think?"

"Isn't that why you think you're in love with Delphia?" Henry asked. "Because she's a Barnes?"

"What did you say?" I kept my volume low even though I wanted to shout at him and then tackle him to the floor.

"Would you have been as infatuated all these years had she been anyone else?" Henry asked. "Isn't it that everyone in this family thinks we're not as good as the Barneses? Aren't we all dedicated to proving that theory is wrong, even to ourselves?"

"Henry, that's enough," Papa said, sharp as a knife.

"You're being very rude," Mama said. "Really, what's gotten into you?"

"We find all the adoration of the Barnes family tedious," Lillian said. "Day in and day out. Now, you'll be courting Delphia, and we'll be subject to it all the more. You know, I don't know if we've had one evening where they didn't come up in conversation."

Two bright pink spots flamed on Henry's cheeks. Did he not care how ill-mannered his wife was being to his family?

"I'm not infatuated with Delphia," I said tightly. "Growing up, she was my best friend, and those feelings developed over time into something deeper. I don't appreciate you making it sound ridiculous."

My brother scowled and gestured toward me with his glass. "Would you worry about what your suit is like if she weren't a Barnes? Or Papa's whiskey there. All for the Barneses. To impress them, to show gratitude. I'm tired of feeling like a charity case."

"We earned every bit of what we have," Mama said. "First by being loyal servants and then by making our own way. How dare you try to make it seem torrid or pathetic in any way."

I'd never in my life heard my mother speak with such anger in her voice. For that matter, Henry's outburst was so unexpected. Had he felt this way all along, or was it anxiety over the war?

45

"Servants, Mama?" Henry asked. "This isn't Victorian England. You were employed by them, not indentured or otherwise." He looked at his wife. "This is exactly what we were talking about."

Talking about? As in, before they came here tonight or many times?

"Helen told us what it was like—dating you," Lillian said. "She knew you were pining over Delphia. I thought she was being paranoid, but I guess she was right. You nearly broke her heart."

"There was nothing nearly about it," I said. "She was in love with a man from back home." Helen and Lillian had been good friends but apparently not close enough to share everything. Otherwise, my sister-in-law would know that Helen pined for her former love. In the end, we had a good chat about it, with me encouraging her to go back home and make it right with him, with or without her father's blessing.

"So you say," Lillian said. "But there was more to it than that. If you'd been truly interested in her things might have been different. She might still be here."

"Helen left to marry her sweetheart back in Georgia. Not that it's any of your business," I said through gritted teeth. "What's it matter to you? You weren't the one who would have had to marry her."

"She was my best friend here." Lillian's gaze darted around the room as if trying to fix on something to steady her emotions. "And now my husband's going to leave to fight a war that has nothing to do with us and leave me all alone."

"You're not alone," Papa said. "You have us. We're your family now."

"My family lives in Denver. I've never been accepted in this town. Everyone still refers to me as Lillian from Denver who dared to marry a Depaul."

Jay, who had stopped playing with his truck, was staring at

his mother. Lillian's combative and sulky tone had scared him. His face crumpled, and he began to cry. My brother picked him up and set him on Lillian's lap. Jay buried his face in her chest.

"This is upsetting the baby," Papa said. "We need to get hold of ourselves."

Mama didn't seem to hear him. "Lillian, no one sees you that way. You haven't put yourself out there. Not really, anyway. You haven't joined any clubs or committees."

"For heaven's sake. The committees," Lillian said, "Always raising money for this or that instead of expecting people to take care of themselves."

Mama brought her hand to her chest and looked as if she might faint. "Lillian, that's unkind of you."

"I don't care," Lillian said. "I miss my family. And now Delphia's back and I'm going to have to endure family holidays with her. It's too much. I want to go back to Denver."

"That's a terrible thing to say," Mama said.

"Well, it's true. If Henry enlists, then I'm moving back to be with my parents."

All color drained out of my mother's face. "You'd take the baby away from us?"

"He's my child," Lillian said. "And my mother has every right to see him as much as you do."

"What about your cottage?" Papa asked. "You'd just up and leave your home?" He didn't mention that he and my mother had given it to them as a wedding gift instead of renting it out. We'd lived there when we were small but had built and moved into the larger house when I was about eight.

"It's not my home," Lillian said. "My mother was right when she told me to put my foot down and tell Henry I wasn't living there."

There was nothing wrong with the cottage. It was small but cozy, perfect for a young family. They were lucky to have a place to move into after they married. Especially once Jay arrived. I'd thought Lillian was quite happy there. The truth was really coming out tonight, and it wasn't pretty.

Did my brother agree about the cottage? If Lillian left with Jay, my mother would be devastated. Especially if both Henry and I were fighting overseas. How selfish of her. I'd never seen this side of her before. Was this her true self, brought out by the news of the day?

"If you don't want to be alone at the cottage," Papa said, "you can both move in here. We have plenty of rooms."

Lillian pursed her lips and shrugged like a sulky child.

"We'll have to talk about it all," Henry said. "And figure out the best solution for the next few months."

My mother was too proud to beg, but I knew losing Jay would be a hard, terrible blow to her heart. She would still be able to see him, I supposed. They could go to Denver to visit him. Maybe Lillian would change her mind later.

I had to get out of there before I said something I regretted. "I've got to go." I went to Mama and gave her a kiss on the cheek. "Please don't wait up. We're going to the club after dinner for dancing."

"Be careful driving," Mama said.

"I will." I nodded toward my father, but I was too angry to look at Henry or Lillian. Regardless, I wasn't about to let them ruin my evening. I'd waited for this night for four and a half years. Whatever bitterness they felt toward Delphia or the Barnes family was of no concern to me. That said, I didn't know Lillian had such spite in her or that my brother felt resentment toward the Barnes family. I had to admit, the argument had shaken me. We couldn't leave it like this. What if the unthinkable happened and one of us didn't make it home? Our last conversation shouldn't be an argument. I'd fix this, I thought. But not tonight. Tonight was for Delphia.

5

DELPHIA

A ddie and I were sitting in the window seat of the bedroom where I'd spent so much of my teenage years. *Bookends.* My mother had described us once this way, and it had stuck with me. We'd come upstairs together after hearing Roosevelt's address over the radio, leaving James downstairs with my father. The two of them loved to talk about books and politics while sharing a drink and a cigar. Disgusting if you ask me. Not the books, mind you, but the cigars.

Snow had fallen all morning, but the skies had cleared around two, and now we could see stars through the window. "I missed this," I said. "Being here with you like this."

"Me too." Addie's legs were spread out long on one side of the bench and mine on the other. We both wore wool stockings, but still, the chilly room made Addie's cheeks pink and pretty. She seemed so happy and content with James and with the success of her writing career. Still, I wondered about children. In our letters back and forth, she'd never mentioned wanting a baby, and I'd not wanted to invade her privacy by asking. I'd have thought she and James would have had a baby by now. They'd been married almost six years. Perhaps they were too

49

busy creating Addie's novels to worry about a human baby? Whatever the reason, she didn't seem bothered by it. Not every woman had to have children to be fulfilled. Like me, for instance.

A tiny voice whispered, *Unless it was with Jack.* I told the voice to be quiet and returned my attention to Addie. She was looking out the window, her expression as dark as the night.

"What is it?" I asked.

"James could be called up," Addie said.

"Surely not? Isn't he too old?" I knew Jack and the twins could be called if they didn't enlist immediately. But James seemed too old.

"He's thirty-four," Addie said. "They already had them sign up for conscription last year. Any men from twenty-one to thirty-four. His number could be picked."

I felt sick. It was bad enough about the twins and Jack, but if we had to send James, too? Dear, gentle James? No, it seemed all wrong.

"Thank God Flynn and Theo are too old, as well as Viktor and Isak and Li," Addie said.

"Will James enlist?"

"No, he told me he won't go unless he's picked."

I thought about that for a moment. If only Jack would decide the same. But he was younger than James. He would see it as his duty to go. Whereas James was older and established in his career. At this point, I couldn't imagine the school running without him. Mama once joked that he couldn't sleep at night unless everyone who graduated from high school could diagram a sentence in their sleep.

"At least for now, anyway," Addie said. "But you know him. He has a strong sense of duty. It's been a struggle for him since Britain declared war on Germany. All the bombings—he's felt every one."

"But he's an American now," I said.

"In some ways, his heart is still in England."

She turned to gaze back out the window. I looked at her reflection in the glass, thinking how beautiful she was.

"Addie?"

"Yes?" She shifted, looking at me with her big blue eyes.

"Why haven't you and James had any children?"

Her eyes looked blank for a moment before she answered casually. "I don't know. Not meant to be, I guess. Theo said it could be because I was so sick when I was a kid."

That seemed unlikely, but I kept that to myself. "Are you sad about it?"

"Not really. I have so many nieces and nephews. My work is kind of like a child."

"As long as you don't mind. Aunt Annabelle minded, and then to lose her child. It was too sad."

"I know, it was. But she's well now, married to her rich husband and living the good life in Florida half the year."

"Thank God they left Paris when they did," I said.

"Annabelle and Bromley could see it coming," Addie said, shuddering. "So awful. Paris falling." Our aunt, who was a famous wedding dress designer, had lost her husband Clive when she was in her thirties. She'd gotten remarried a few years later to a man she'd met years earlier and never forgotten. I'd had a little something to do with it all, helping her coordinate leaving town without telling anyone she was returning to Florida where she'd met Bromley while still married to Clive. Nothing untoward had happened when Clive was still with us, but she'd felt something for Bromley, even though she loved her husband. After Clive died, she received a letter from Bromley asking if she would like to see him again. She didn't tell anyone but me where she was going. My mother was aghast and worried but soon got over it when Annabelle came home married and happy.

"I know. It all seemed so far away. Until yesterday."

"Yes. I feel the same," I said.

"Tell me about this date with Jack," Addie said, smiling. "And the drive home from the station yesterday."

I'd mentioned to Addie earlier that Jack had asked me out on a date but nothing else. I didn't want my whole family to know, or I'd have been teased relentlessly. She knew me, though. She'd known my feelings for him before I left for college. In fact, she'd been concerned I would give up the idea of school and stay to be with him. No chance for that, I'd assured her. I wanted a higher education more than anything else.

"Well, he told me that this Helen person meant nothing to him," I said.

"I figured that out myself."

"How so?"

"I saw them together a few times at the club," Addie said. "He never looked at her the way he looks at you."

"Am I a terrible person that this makes me happy?"

Addie laughed. "In matters of the heart, sometimes, we must be ruthless."

"Have you been happy with James? Is marriage what you hoped it would be?"

"Oh yes. I adore that man. He's the only one in the world for me. We have the most wonderful life together. I love being close to Papa and Mama." Since I'd been gone, they built a beautiful brick house not far from here. Every day, Addie walked over to see our mother for coffee or tea and a chat about whatever she was working on or gossip about our family. They'd written to me separately about what a joy it was to have the chance to spend time together. I'd been a little jealous. Nothing new, of course. Addie and our mother were similar and had much in common. Whereas I was more like Papa—seeking adventure and rebelling against whatever the world seemed to want me to do. However, he'd settled down here with Mama and all their children just fine. Perhaps I could too. With Jack? "Yesterday—

52

the drive home—was the most romantic thing that's ever happened to me."

"Tell me everything," Addie said. "Every word."

"Will you put it in a book?" I narrowed my eyes, pretending to be worried.

"I might. It depends on how romantic it really is." She grinned, playing with the string of pearls around her neck. They were a lovely contrast to her dark purple dress. She and James were staying for dinner with our parents, who still asked us to dress formally for dinner. "I'm thinking of writing a love story next."

I laughed. "Well, he said the most remarkable thing—he'd been waiting for me to come home and that only I would do. Or something like that."

Her face shone with delight. "Oh my, well, that is romantic. How did you feel when he said such a bold thing?"

How had I felt? Warm. Alive. Joyful. "I felt a buzz of excitement that went from my head to my toes. It was like a good dream."

"I always thought you two would end up together, but then you went away and he was dating Helen. I worried you two were walking away from your true destinies."

"Is destiny all about the person you marry?" Was that all I was supposed to worry about in this life? What about ambition and success?

"No, not really. It's just that the person you choose to make a life with affects every single other thing. Without the right partner, you can't become who you're supposed to be."

"Unless you remain single. Then you can do whatever it is you wish to do and have no one to answer to but yourself."

"Is that what you want?" Addie's eyes widened, and she bit her bottom lip. She did this when she worried, which was often when it came to me. She wanted me to be happy and feared I would never be.

"I want to make my own way and not rely on a man."

"You can do that and be happily married," Addie said simply. "Look at James and me."

"True enough."

"Promise me you'll give love a chance. Don't dismiss it to make a point or whatever it is your rebellious nature is inclined to do."

I laughed, resting my head against the wall. "I promise I will. Jack makes it easy to imagine what it would be like to be loved by him for my whole life."

"That's what I want to hear." She beamed at me, obviously thrilled.

For a moment, we sat quietly, easy with each other as only sisters can be. She knew everything about me, flaws and gifts and everything in between. Addie was a safe haven for me and always had been, even when I was naughty as a child.

"Do you remember how I insisted Viktor be the one to find my husband?" I asked.

"Sure. It was the cutest thing."

"He told me before I left for college that he'd choose Jack for me if it was up to him."

"Really? You never told me that."

"He also said that if it were meant to be, our time would come. Viktor always encouraged me to be myself and if that meant college, then I should pursue it first."

"Good advice."

"When I left, I didn't think Jack would wait. I didn't even think he felt that way about me."

"He didn't want to get in your way. That's my guess anyway," Addie said.

"That's what he told me yesterday."

She gestured toward my old cotton dress I'd pulled on while fixing my hair and makeup. "Isn't it time to get you dressed? What are you wearing tonight? It has to be special."

I unfolded from the window seat and went to the wardrobe to show her the dress I'd chosen for the occasion—a Grecian draped gown in light blue silk. With the filmy sleeves and layered skirt, the gown was pretty while being modest at the same time. It was important to my mother that I not appear cheap in any way. College was one thing, but one must remain a lady, even in these modern times.

"It's beautiful," Addie said. "Do you want me to help you into it?"

"Yes, please."

She held it while I stepped into the dress, then zipped me up. My girdle felt a tad loose, but it would still give me a smooth silhouette under the dress. I'd lost weight the last few months working for that awful beady-eyed man. He'd made me so nervous I'd not been able to get much lunch down. By the time I returned to the boardinghouse in the evenings, I fell into bed exhausted.

"You've grown awfully thin," Addie said as her gaze swept over me. "But now that you're home, Lizzie will fatten you up."

"Nothing tastes as good as her food." I'd noticed Lizzie seemed tired since I'd returned. She was in her sixties now, having had a child later in life than most women of her generation. Our butler and Papa's valet, Jasper, had taken decades to figure out that he and Lizzie were meant to be. Florence, their daughter, who had grown up with us, had married a doctor from back east somewhere and from her letters and Lizzie's accounts, they seemed very happy together.

I sat at the dressing table to put on lipstick. I'd already put makeup and powder on earlier, as well as a layer of mascara. My hair had been coaxed into smooth finger waves in the front and large rolled curls in the back. I'd gone to the salon that morning, needing a good set and style before my date. I'd been surprised to see several new girls working at the hair shop. Emerson Pass might be in the mountains, but the ladies still liked their hair washed and set every week. What would happen to us if all the young men went to war? Would we still care about our hair?

"Can you put all this talk of war away for the night?" Addie asked from the easy chair next to the dressing table. "And enjoy yourself with Jack?"

"I'll have to. We've been waiting a long time for this."

I stood, smoothing my dress. "Will I do?"

"Yes, my baby sister. You'll do."

JACK ARRIVED PROMPTLY AT SEVEN. I was still upstairs fastening my shoes when we heard a vehicle pull into the driveway. I scurried over to the window. In the darkness, he was barely visible as he crossed the yard to our front porch.

Addie offered to tell him I'd be down in a moment. A girl liked to make a grand entrance, after all. I knew, too, that Papa would make him sit with him for a few moments, asking questions about where we were going and how late we intended to be.

Upon entering the sitting room, I saw Papa, James, and Jack huddled over a map of Europe spread out across the surface of the coffee table. They both straightened when I entered and headed toward them. From the couch, Mama smiled when she saw me and gave me a slight nod of approval.

Jack's expression was one of admiration. He reached out to take my hand and bring it up to his mouth for a kiss. In our long friendship, he'd never once done that. We were all grown up now, I thought. Ready for the next season of our relationship.

"You're stunning," Jack said. "There are no words for what you are, actually. Not that I know of, anyway."

He looked pretty spectacular himself, wearing a dark brown wool suit that made his blue eyes pop. His hair, parted on the side, a little longer in the front, and styled with pomade, made an attractive dip over his forehead. "You look like you could be in the picture shows," I said. He could, with those gleaming white teeth of his and strong jawline.

He held up his hands. "Nah, I'm a working man and have the callouses to show for it."

A shiver of desire crept up my spine. The pads of his hands were thick from years of wrangling horses and baling hay and whatever else had to be done to keep their farm going. I could easily imagine them running up the length of my bare arms. Or legs. *Oh my, I mustn't think of those things or Papa will lock me up,* I thought.

"Nothing wrong with that," Papa said, referring to Jack's callouses. "Would you care for a drink before you go?"

"No, sir. I want my mind clear for driving," Jack said. "The stars are out, but it's a dark night."

"Good man." My father clasped him on the shoulder.

Jack and James shook hands, as if they hadn't just seen each other, most likely in town or church, only a short time ago. "Have a good time. Try to forget the war for a night anyway," James said.

"I'll do my best," Jack said.

I went over to kiss Mama goodbye and whisper thanks to Addie for helping me dress.

"Have a nice time, darling," Mama said.

Jasper arrived in the sitting room announcing dinner would be ready in five minutes.

"Time for us to take our leave then," Jack said. "May I help you on with your coat?"

"Yes, please." I'd placed my best wool coat by the door. I already had gloves on, a pair of silky white ones I saved for best.

In the foyer, he helped me into my long wool coat. His thumb brushed the inside of my arm, and even through the pair of long gloves, my skin warmed under his touch. A flutter in my stomach seemed to emphasize the point. I was terribly attracted to this man. Who wouldn't be?

"I've borrowed my father's car, so you won't have to bounce around the cab of the truck," he said as he opened the door for me.

"How thoughtful of you."

He hung on to the side of the door, peering down at me in the light from our porch lamp. "God save me, you are a beauty."

"Thank you. It's nice to have a night out and an excuse to dress up."

He shut the door of the car and then sprinted around the front. He'd put his own overcoat on as well, and it swirled between his ankles and kneecaps. Around his neck, a bright red scarf made him look festive. He took my breath away. When he got into the car, I smelled his spicy shaving soap and a hint of the outdoors. Jack's smell. How I loved it. I'd almost forgotten how much.

Once we were making our way down the driveway, I tried to breathe more easily, but it was hard. I felt breathless. I was putting too much stock in tonight, I thought. It was this war hanging over everything and giving it all more weight than it should have. We should be enjoying our first date, not wondering if it would be only one of a handful we would have before he left. Or if he never came back, leaving me with only memories.

"Will we be able to talk of anything but the war tonight?" Jack asked in the relative darkness. It would be unlikely that we'd meet any other cars until we got out to the main road.

"I'd like to. But I don't know if it's possible, given today."

"Well, we should make a pact to try at least. We have four years to catch up on."

That wasn't quite accurate. We'd seen each other a few times in the last few years, including at a Christmas party last year. I'd not come home again after that, going to work for the professor right after graduation. I'd hoped Jack would write, but he never had. At the time, I figured he was too busy courting that Helen woman around town. Now that I knew he'd never ceased thinking about me, I could see it all with fresh eyes. This was the beginning of something important. Perhaps the most important relationship I would ever have. One day at a time, I reminded myself. Wedding bells were not ringing yet. Hitler would make sure of that.

6

JACK

It was one of those spectacularly clear nights we have in the winter, with stars glowing from an inky sky. The air, although below freezing, was still without the stinging wind we sometimes had. Freshly fallen snow blanketed everything but the roads, which had been plowed that morning. They would be slick with ice, so I drove cautiously.

Between the hum of the engine and my concentration on the road, we didn't talk much on the way to the lodge where I had a dinner reservation made. Finally, we arrived, and a few minutes later, our coats and my hat had been checked and we were sitting at a table by the window. It was a Monday night, thus uncrowded in the formal dining room. Not only a Monday but *the* Monday we went to war. People were at home, listening to the radio and worrying.

"How's your mother? Mine's a wreck," Delphia said after we'd ordered the roast beef dinner special.

"She's scared. Papa, too." I hadn't planned to share the tale of my family and the tension that the war had evoked between us, but soon the story was tumbling out of my mouth. Delphia and I were old friends and knew each other's families well. She was as shocked as I'd been by Henry's and Lillian's resentment about the Barnes family in relation to our own. "All these years, he's felt like my father gave too much credence to yours. I had no idea he felt all those things. About your family or ours. I have a feeling it's Lillian's opinion more than his."

Delphia looked down at the napkin on her lap. "I can understand his feelings."

"Henry's?" We were seated in a booth and had naturally gravitated toward the center. Our thighs were only inches from each other. I had to keep my head straight and my hands to myself. "Why?"

"It would grow old to hear about how my father saved yours and all that, and make a person feel as if they weren't seen as equals. Which my father would hate, by the way. His generosity was out of the kindness of his heart but also a selfish desire to give fine people opportunities to make our community strong in values and integrity. Your father was one of those men. Papa saw something special in him, or he wouldn't have gifted him with the land."

"I've always wondered about it," I said. "I've never been sure I could ever be that giving. However, it makes sense the way you've described it. Henry might benefit from that perspective."

"None of us were at our best today. How could we be expected to be? I'll bet he apologizes tomorrow."

"We're all tense, that's for certain," I said.

Our salads arrived, crisp lettuce covered with a vinaigrette. We dived in, eating instead of talking for a few minutes. When my plate was empty, I watched her for a moment, smitten with the way she took small, dainty bites, reminding me of a bird.

She looked up and blushed. "What?"

"I like the way you eat."

"That's ridiculous."

"I know," I said, grinning. "But I can't help myself. You're so pretty and smell nice and I can't believe you're here."

"I can't believe you're here either," she said. "But it's about time, I think."

"You know, you're generous, like your father. Thinking of Henry kindly when he and Lillian were acting awful is the perfect example."

"Their hostility isn't really about my father or our family," Delphia said. "It's about how Henry feels about himself, which I pity but also understand. I'm the last of a line of successful Barnes children. I feel pressure to be as great as the rest of them, only I don't have a talent like each of them."

"I seem to recall you being the cleverest in the whole school." I waved a tomato wedge at her. "You'll be smart at business, like your father. You'll see, Delphia Barnes. Someday, you might even surprise yourself."

She smiled back at me. "I hope you're right."

I hesitated, hating to spoil the mood, but it had to be said. "I'm enlisting tomorrow. Beaumont and Bleu are going with me into Denver to sign up."

"I figured as much." She pushed the remaining lettuce around the plate. "I wish we had more time."

I reached across and took her hand. "I'll come back. Don't worry. My father raised me tough."

"I know he did. But I'll be worried just the same."

The rest of dinner was pleasant as we reminisced and filled each other in on the four and a half years she was away. I told her of our changes at the farm and that with my brother and me both working for my father, we were able to breed more horses and expand into markets we hadn't foreseen, such as competitive horses for racing. "Mostly it's been my ideas—if I can say that without sounding boastful. Papa is averse to risk, as is Henry, but I've been able to convince them to take the leap as new opportunities arise. Without us to help, though, I don't know how much Papa can do alone."

"He may have to hire some women," I said. "Like a lot of other businesses in town."

That led us to talk about the nightclub and the ideas Delphia had to improve it. "Once Li and Fiona stopped playing there, the quality of music went down. I want to recruit musicians from all over the country, booking them for short stints. With advertising, we can start to create a name for ourselves as a venue for good music and dancing, as well as the best cocktails around."

"What does your mother think about all this?" I couldn't picture Quinn Barnes being a proponent of her daughter managing a nightclub.

"She hasn't said much," Delphia said. "She knows Flynn and Phillip want to disengage from the day-to-day operations. They don't trust anyone outside of the family to run things, thus they're stuck with me. Flynn agrees with my strategy but doesn't have the time or inclination to put that much work into it. He's older now, and the girls and Shannon need him at home in the evenings. Phillip's had less to do with the club, but he's excited to step away as well."

"Delphia Barnes, nightclub owner. I like it."

"It seems like I should be a crusty battle-ax with a cigarette hanging out of my mouth," Delphia said.

"No, you're the stunningly beautiful variety of nightclub owners. They're all the rage, from what I hear."

Her eyes sparkled at me. "Are you ready to dance with me, Jack?"

"I was born ready."

WE SPENT the better part of an hour out on the dance floor. Delphia had learned a lot of new dances while away at school.

TESS THOMPSON

"We danced with each other to learn how to swing dance," she said. "So if I lead, don't be insulted."

A local band was playing. They were all right, but I missed the days when Fiona and Li had played all the popular music of the times. The dance floor wasn't full tonight by any means, so we had a lot of space to twirl around the room with abandon.

The lack of crowds and mediocre music didn't matter. We were having too much fun to care. In addition to swing dancing, we did the Charleston, a well-known one from our youth, the jitterbug, and the jive. Delphia was an expert dancer, but I did well enough to be able to keep up with her. Finally, after an hour with no break, I dragged her to our table and begged her for a respite and a drink.

Laughing, she agreed, fanning her face with her hands. "It *is* a little warm."

I ordered us gin rickeys—her choice—and we settled back into the booth. Should I put my arm around her? We'd touched a lot during dancing and she seemed to like it, but who knew? The last thing I wanted was for her to feel any pressure. She might be a bit of a rebel when it came to a woman's role in the workforce, but she was still a Barnes, old-fashioned and proper. Her mother had taught her well, as had mine. There were parts of America where young people might play their morals fast and loose, but here in Emerson Pass, we still believed in a long courtship. Too bad I didn't have all the time in the world to win her heart. From what I'd heard this afternoon in town, once we enlisted, we'd be sent off to basic training a week or so later. America needed to build up our troops fast. There would be no time for dallying or dancing.

"What is it?" Delphia asked, bringing a napkin to her throat to wipe away the dampness from our rigorous exercise.

"I wish I didn't have to go. You've just come home."

"I've been trying not to think of it," she said.

"I'm not planning on dying."

"If anyone has a chance of making it back here alive, it's you." She set aside her napkin and scooted closer to me. The sides of the booth were wide and long, making me feel as if we were in a cocoon or maybe a nest.

Under the tablecloth, I searched for her hand, taking it in mine and giving it a good squeeze. "I have a lot to come home to, don't I?"

"I'll be here," she said. "However long it takes."

"Are you sure? Do you really want to promise me you'll wait? We've only had one date."

"That's how much I'd like a second one." Her mouth twitched into a smile, but her eyes were sad and sweet. "Jack, haven't we waited long enough to admit our feelings?"

My heart surged with joyful hope. She wanted me. After all this time, I finally had Delphia. "I believe we have."

"Let's not waste any more time being subtle. You're the only one for me."

"You're the only one for me," I said.

The server brought our drinks, but we hardly noticed him. We both took a sip of the fizzy drink, but neither of us really cared about the booze.

"I wish I'd told you how I felt sooner," I said.

"You were right to wait. I wasn't ready yet. I needed to do things my own way and come back when I was ready."

"And you're ready now?" I asked. "To give me a chance?"

"It's not a chance you need. I'm telling you outright—I love you. I think I always have."

The angels seemed to sing for me then in a great swell of glorious sound only I could hear. She loved me. My dream girl loved me back. How had I ever doubted her? "I love you too." I removed my hand from hers to caress the side of her face, not caring who saw us. "You're the only one I can picture spending my life with."

"Because of my superior dancing?" Delphia looked into my

eyes, and the emotion I saw shining back at me caused my chest to ache.

"Your dancing, your mind, your heart. All of it makes you the woman I want next to me." I brushed my thumb across her mouth, smearing her lipstick. "I've smudged your makeup," I whispered in her ear. "But I can't think about anything else but kissing you."

She glanced around us. The band had taken a break, so the room was quieter than it had been. A few couples were in the other booths, not paying a bit of attention to us, perhaps soaking up these last moments as we were. Soon, this town would be empty of young lovers, leaving only the women behind. It would be a burden and hard, waiting for their men to come home. What choice did any of us have, though? This was the trial of our generation and we must bear it, just as our ancestors had since the beginning of time. Courage. That's what it would take to walk away from the only life I'd ever known. My horses and my family and friends. Hardest of all to leave would be the woman sitting here, staring up at me with love plastered across her face and glittering in her eyes.

"Since no one's paying the least attention to us," Delphia said, "I think even my mother would approve of a kiss. This is our first real date, after all, but not even close to the first time we've enjoyed each other's company."

I'd gotten a little lost during that short speech. Did she want me to kiss her or not?

As if I'd asked the question out loud, she nodded. "Yes, you may kiss me now."

"In my daydreams, it was under the stars," I said, teasing her.

"That can be our third kiss."

I laughed, delighted by her clever and quick responses. She'd always been the smartest person I'd ever known. Smarter than me, but that was all right. She didn't seem to notice. I kissed her, lingering softly at her mouth, tasting her with the tip of my tongue. When we broke apart, my eyes stung. I loved this woman. How could I be apart from her again? It would be excruciating to have to leave her behind when we were finally getting started.

She tilted her head, watching me. "Kissing is as good as everyone says."

I smiled. "I thought I knew what kissing was, but now I can see that I knew nothing. Kissing you is different from anything I've done before."

Her eyes sparkled. "I'm glad to hear you've forgotten your kisses with Helen."

"Who's Helen?" I asked deadpan. "My heart knows only one woman, and her name is Delphia Barnes." I leaned close to kiss her again. Goodness, she tasted as sweet as she looked. I wanted to devour her, drag her back home to my bed. But this is not how things were done. We would wait until marriage. Would she marry me at some point? I had to believe she would, or I would lose my mind.

"Through the years, my sisters have told me how it was for them when they first fell in love." Delphia plucked at the lapel of my suit jacket. "How they knew he was the one for them. Now I know what they meant. The idea of living life without you is impossible. Which means you have to stay alive and well."

I grinned, the ache in my chest coming from equal measures love and angst at having to leave her. "I wish I didn't have to go," I said.

"The idea of this town being without Jack Depaul is hard for me to fathom. But I'll go on just the same, hoping you'll be home sooner rather than later. And all in one piece." She waggled a finger at me and spoke with a lilt in her voice. "I don't want you injured, do you hear me?" Although I understood she was only joking, I knew what she meant. So many of the men who came back from the First World War had scars of the spirit, not visible to the outside world but internally devastating.

"We could marry before I leave," I said casually, as if I'd only just thought of it. "Spend the next few weeks together."

She stared at me. The idea had obviously not occurred to her before now. "Get married? Now?"

"Never mind. Silly idea." I flushed with humiliation. Why had I mentioned marriage when we were on our first date?

"It's too soon. Isn't that right?" Delphia asked. "Won't that be what everyone says?"

"Yes, of course, it is. I'm sorry. I'm an idiot to bring it up."

"Not an idiot," she said. "But I don't know that rushing into something is a good idea."

"You're right. Obviously," I said. It wasn't really obvious to me, but I was clearly further ahead than she.

"Eloping *is* romantic, and while I love the idea, it's not exactly what I would hope for."

"What do you mean?"

"Married in haste and all that? People would talk. Which, of course, makes me want to do it all the more. My family would not think it was a good idea. Can you imagine if I told them tomorrow morning that we were marrying before you left? They'd think we'd gone mad."

"Maybe we are a little. Madly in love?"

"They wouldn't think of it like that," Delphia said. "My mother, especially, would be worried we were jumping into it too quickly."

"Mine might think it was too hasty, as well," I admitted. "However, I'm thinking of the time we have left before I leave."

Her eyes widened. "Are you talking about man-and-wife activities?"

I laughed. "I suppose I am."

"We are old enough to know what we want, I suppose." Delphia tugged at the string of shiny beads around her neck. "It might be best to elope and beg forgiveness later."

"Yes. We could just do it and tell everyone afterward," I said.

"There's nothing anyone can do after that. I mean, why not? It's our life, our decision."

She shook her head, making her sparkly earrings bounce like headlights on a dirt road. "Maybe for others, but I'm a Barnes. We don't elope. We get married at the house and everyone gives speeches and dances to Fiona and Li's music. My parents would be disappointed, not to mention my sisters. Aunt Annabelle would be deprived of making a special wedding dress for me. She's made one for all of my sisters and my mother, too."

I put my hands up, laughing. "All good points. It was only an idea."

"But we would have a few weeks together as man and wife before you left." Her cheeks blazed pink, obviously thinking of all the fun we could have as married people. "Memories we could live on for however long you're away."

"I like that idea," I said.

"Me too. We could compromise and do a small, quick wedding at the house. Something easy and without fuss. This is wartime. My family will appreciate that timing is not on our side."

"Are we insane?" I asked.

"Probably." She grinned. "But when have you or I done anything but exactly what we please? We live how we want. It's one of the things we have in common."

"Agreed."

"You'll have to ask Papa, though. That's a tradition we can't ignore, or he'll be heartbroken."

"I wouldn't think of doing anything else." I hoped he would give his blessing. If not, I was the one who would be heartbroken.

7

DELPHIA

The next morning, I woke feeling rested, as if I'd slept on a happy cloud. Jack and I were getting married. It was a bold move, yes, but I felt deep in my bones that marrying Jack was the right thing to do. We'd been friends for such a long time. We knew our hearts and that we didn't want to waste another moment. However, as blissfully happy as I was, the awful thought that he might not come back to me gave me pause. Young men were dying every minute in Europe.

I dressed and went downstairs for breakfast. Mama and Papa were already in the dining room. Papa, as he did every morning, was scouring the newspaper. Mama was staring out the window, seemingly lost in thought.

She sent me a distracted smile. "Did you have a nice time last night, darling?"

"I did." I helped myself to a cup of coffee and one of Lizzie's scones along with a dollop of raspberry jam. Once I'd sat in my usual spot, I took a better look at Mama. Pale and red-eyed, she seemed completely out of sorts. "Mama, did something happen?"

0

Papa put down his newspaper to look at me. "We've had some bad news, I'm afraid."

My heart started beating faster and felt as if it were between my ears. Was it Beaumont and Bleu? Had they announced their intention to enlist?

"Your brother Theo came by last night after you left," Mama said, voice trembling. "They're calling him up. They need doctors."

"But he's too old," I blurted out. "Isn't he?"

"They don't care how old they are—it's his medical degree they care about."

"Oh, I see." Shaken, under the table, I wrapped my cloth napkin around my hand. Not Theo. Of all of us, he was the least suited for war. He'd already served once. During the Great War, he and Flynn had lied about their age so they could enlist. Theo had come home battered mentally. Mama said he struggled for quite some time with nightmares and anxiety. Studying medicine and throwing himself into healing whoever needed care in our small community was his way of coping.

Between him and Dr. Neal, there wasn't a person in our town who hadn't been touched in some way by their small practice. How would Dr. Neal do it alone, with only Louisa to help? I didn't ask that question, not wanting to worry Mama further.

"When does he have to go?" I asked instead.

"He has a few weeks," Papa said.

"Poor Louisa and Simon," I said under my breath. Louisa was a wonderful wife and mother, but she relied on Theo, as he did her, to provide a sense of safety and predictability. After her tumultuous childhood, no one could blame her for that. Theo, being sensitive of nature, needed her steadying presence as well. They provided each other the refuge they both craved. Parting them seemed too cruel. Especially since Theo had already served.

"Flynn's going, too." Mama's eyes filled. "He refuses to see

71

reason, saying only that he and Theo should stick together. They had in the first war, and they would now."

"He blames himself for Theo's troubles," Papa said to me, as if I didn't know that. Flynn had been the one to convince Theo.

Flynn came home with ideas for a ski resort. Theo came home with anxiety attacks.

"Surely he knows he could do more good here with his wife and daughters," I said, referring to Flynn.

"He doesn't know that," Mama said. "And he's stubborn, so there's no convincing him."

"He'll go in as an officer," Papa said. "But there's no guarantee he'll be anywhere near Theo."

"Theo will be safer than a soldier," Mama said. "But a commanding officer will be out with his troops." She dabbed her eyes. "I can't stand it. Not again. I won't be able to sleep until they return to us."

"To further add to our worries, Fiona rang first thing this morning," Papa said. "The twins plan to enlist as well."

"Jack, too," I said. "They're going together."

Mama closed her eyes as if her head hurt. "How can we be stupid enough to be doing this again? I'd kill Hitler with my own hands if I could."

Papa and I gaped at her. She'd never said anything of the sort. At least not that I'd ever heard.

"I'm sorry," Mama said. "But God help me, I can't reconcile this. Not again."

"Are you all right?" Papa asked me gently. "About Jack?"

"I'm not all right, but I know there's no talking him out of it. These boys, the ones who grew up here, they're patriotic and they're brave."

"We have no one to blame but ourselves for that," Papa said with a jocularity I know he didn't feel.

"No, it's true," Mama said. "We taught them well. No

cowards here. And now their mothers and sisters and wives have to watch them march right into danger."

"What if it were the other way, though?" I asked. "Wouldn't we be ashamed of them if they weren't willing to defend their country and freedom?"

Mama sighed and dabbed at the corners of her eyes again. "You're right, darling, but still—I'm terrified."

"I am, too," I said softly. "But we have to be as brave as them."

Mama nodded. "We'll jump into the war effort here at home, you and me. There's all kinds of things we can do to help."

"I won't be knitting socks," I said. "Or the boys will have holes in the toes."

That got a small, sad smile out of my mother. "You'll have to find another way to help."

"How was last night?" Papa asked. "Tell us something happy."

I started in on the club and some of the things I'd noticed and wanted to change, like the music and the lighting, as well as adding more modern cocktails to the menu.

"Not that, dear," Papa said. "The date with Jack. Did you have a good time?"

"Oh, yes. Very much." I smiled, remembering the kisses we'd shared in the car and then on the front porch. "In fact, he'd like to come see you this afternoon, if that's all right."

My parents exchanged a glance.

"Is this what you want?" Papa asked me. "Marriage? This is fast."

"We've been friends all our lives," I said. "He's who I want— the only one I've ever loved. And we want to marry before he leaves for basic training."

"But that's only weeks away," Mama said, sounding wounded. "How would we be able to plan anything in such a short amount of time?"

"Something simple, Mama. Here at the house, with cake and

73

punch and maybe some dancing. Fiona and Li could play music for us."

Mama took a good, long look at me. "Are you sure this is right? Marrying in haste is never a good idea, and you've only just come home."

"I want to send him off as his wife, not just a girl back home." A lump gathered at the back of my throat, momentarily keeping me from speaking.

"Jack is one of the finest young men we know," Papa said. "And if he's the one you want, then you shall have our blessing. We've prayed for this news for a long time now."

"You have?" I asked.

"We've felt you and Jack were just the right match," Mama said. "I was particularly impressed by how he refrained from putting his own desires above yours."

"He never said anything to me about his feelings," I said. "In fact, I thought he was going to marry that Helen person."

"That poor girl couldn't hold a candle to you, my dearest," Papa said.

"Thank you, Papa." I choked back tears, touched by his words. "Mama, we'll just have his family and ours for the wedding party. We can marry at the church and then come back here for bubbles and cake."

"No, that won't do. We'll have a feast," Mama said. "Lizzie and I can figure out a menu." She started counting off on her fingers how many guests there would be. "There's our giant clan and then four of them. Lizzie and Jasper, of course. They wouldn't want to miss it, having put up with you all these years."

Papa and I caught each other's gaze. This would be good for Mama. Planning a wedding, albeit a small one, would be a good distraction as she waited for her sons and grandsons to be taken away from her.

"You may tell your young man to come by this afternoon,"

Papa said. "We'll have a chat, as I've done with all of your sisters' suitors."

I got up to give Papa and then Mama a hug. "It will all be well," I said to Mama. "God will keep them safe."

"I hope you're right." She cupped my face with her two small hands. "Now, go on. You better tell your sisters that we need an emergency meeting at teatime. We have a wedding to plan."

THAT NIGHT, my siblings, Bleu, and Beaumont gathered for dinner in our formal dining room. The rest of the nieces and nephews were downstairs in the kitchen enjoying a raucous dinner supervised by Lizzie. But the remainder of us were seated around our long dining room table. Li and Fiona sat together, pale and nervous. Viktor and Cymbeline, looking fit and healthy, sat next to each other, both obviously trying to keep the conversation from becoming too serious by making jokes and asking questions. James and Addie huddled close together, always touching, even if it were only shoulder to shoulder.

Theo, grave-faced when he arrived, had loosened up some, although Louisa was quieter than usual. Flynn and Shannon were overly jolly, hiding the tension his decision had caused their young family. Finally, there were Josephine and dear Phillip, who never ceased to move me with his obvious love of our family. Even after all these years, he seemed never to forget what it was like to have no family and then marry into ours. Even if we sometimes took for granted the close-knit family we had, he never did. I loved him for it as well as for his kind and thoughtful treatment of my sister and their daughters.

Over roast duck and several bottles from Papa's stash of delicious French wine, we talked of everything but war. Josephine, who typically was as straitlaced as they came, had several glasses of 1910 Bordeaux and began telling funny stories of the family when they were all young, including recollections of Mama and Papa's wedding day.

"You know, I was almost fourteen by then," Jo said, "and thought of myself as quite mature."

"You weren't that much younger than I," Mama said. "Yet you'd taken care of all your sisters and brothers like a grown woman."

"Maybe that's why I thought of myself as so grown up," Jo said. "But what a relief it was to hand them all over to you, Mama. I was able to be a kid again."

"I can remember the day she arrived like it was yesterday," Papa said. "Do you remember?" he asked the group collectively.

"It's one of my earliest memories," Fiona said. "I thought she was a princess."

"I thought she was dead," Cym said.

Mama laughed. "When I woke up to all of you surrounding me, I thought I was in heaven with the angels."

"We were hardly angels," Flynn said. "Especially Cym."

"It takes one to know one," Cym said, making a face at our mischievous brother.

"We took one look at her," Jo said, "and decided she needed to be our new mother, regardless of whatever Papa wanted. I never thought about what he wanted."

"I agreed with your assessment," Papa said, laughing.

"We'd run away a few nannies by then." Flynn grinned, as if the memories of his naughtiness tickled him to this day. "Mostly because of the clever ideas. The frog incident of 1910, for example."

"You children were terrible to those poor women," Mama said.

"They were not poor women," Theo said. "Hideous, every one of them."

"Good nannies were hard to find," Papa said. "Especially

when you Barnes children had such a bad reputation. Word of the frog in the bed got around quick."

"One time Flynn had this grand idea to drop a bucket of water on one of their heads," Jo said. "In the middle of the night. We had it all rigged up, but there was a flaw in the engineering and it ended up all over poor Lizzie instead. She was so mad at us."

"Not for long," Cym said. "She could never stay mad at us for too long."

"To Lizzie," Papa said, raising his glass.

We all raised ours, murmuring our love and appreciation for the woman who had dedicated so much of her life to caring for us and was doing so now with all the children downstairs.

"And to your dear grandmother," Mama said, gesturing to Li. "May she rest in peace."

Tears stung my eyes at the thought of Mrs. Wu. She'd lived to be ninety if she was a day—no one knew her exact age—and had passed away in her sleep from old age. The best way to go, I thought now, but that didn't mean we didn't miss her. She and Lizzie had worked together for twenty years in the kitchen, complementing each other's strengths.

"Thank you," Li said, bobbing his shiny head of black hair. "She had a good life here with all of us. As did I. She said to me the day before she passed how blessed we'd been to be allowed into your home."

"She gave much more than she took," Mama said. "I still think she saved Theo's life that time when he was so sick."

Li smiled his gentle smile. "She thought so too. Never one to keep her opinion about the power of herbs to herself."

"I miss her every day," Addie said softly. "She was always so good to me, making sure I had special things to eat when all of you were having dishes made with flour."

"She loved you all," Li said.

"Your family really has a knack for picking up stray cats,

77

doesn't it?" Beaumont asked cheekily. "Little boys from France included."

"We weren't at all sure we'd be able to do right by you," Fiona said. "I was much too young to be raising little boys."

Bleu and Beaumont, who were identical twins, were handsome young men with shocks of dark curls and dancing eyes. Like my brothers, they were alike but different at the same time, with Beaumont being the more outgoing of the two. Their future plans for their business would have to wait until after the war. How long would we have to wait? No one could answer this question, even though we wished we could.

"But you did magnificently," Mama said to Fiona. "All of my girls are wonderful mothers."

"With a lot of help, but thank you, Mama. Thank goodness for you, or with five children, I would not be able to enjoy my musical work. I'm lucky." Fiona glanced fondly at her adult twins. "I enjoyed every minute of being your mother. And now look at you—all grown up. Off to fight in a war we have nothing to do with." Her voice cracked. I was next to her and saw Li reach into her lap to hold her hand.

"We'll be fine, Mother," Bleu said to Fiona. "Those Nazis will be sorry they messed with us."

"I certainly hope so," Fiona said.

"Anyway, the war has *everything* to do with us now," Beaumont said. "Japan shouldn't have bombed us. They'll have to pay for it. Once we get over there, we'll end this thing. Regardless, we're all connected in this world. People deserve to be free, and the dictators of the world must answer for their tyranny. We cannot let our fellow human beings suffer, can we? If we can help—we must. Isn't that what you taught us, Mother?"

"I suppose it is," Fiona said, a mixture of sadness and pride in her voice.

"We should open another bottle of this." Papa gestured

toward the empty bottle of wine in an obvious attempt to change the subject.

And so we did, carrying on for the rest of the night as if the war didn't lurk nearby like a nasty black cloud. In our formal parlor, Fiona and Li shared with us some sections from their latest musical score. She played the piano and he accompanied with his violin in a haunting melody that sent chills up and down my spine and made goose bumps on my arms.

After the concert, Theo and Louisa left to help a woman in town have her first baby. Their son, Simon, had a cold and had not been able to make it to dinner. Li and Fiona, obviously exhausted, begged off as well, rounding up their younger children from downstairs.

We put a jazz record on the phonograph. No one was in the mood for dancing, but the ladies pulled out decks of cards and we played gin while the men went to the sitting room to play poker.

It was nearing eleven by the time everyone left. I was bleary-eyed by then and looking forward to my bed. Once I was between the sheets with the feather comforter tucked around my body, I closed my eyes and fell into a sleep plagued with nightmares of bombs and gunfire.

8

JACK

That morning, I made sure to finish my chores as quickly as I could so I could spend time with my parents at lunch. Henry always went home to Lillian for the midday meal, leaving me the chance to speak with them alone. They already knew I'd joined the marines. Now I needed to make my intention to marry Delphia known. It would not be a negotiation of any kind. I knew what I wanted. If my parents didn't give their blessing, I would do it anyway. Delphia and I knew our own hearts and minds.

Our cook had made a hearty lentil and pork soup served with chunks of fresh bread and butter. The three of us sat together in the dining room. Our house had the kitchen on the ground floor. While we were enjoying our lunch, the staff would have theirs in the kitchen. We only had a cook, one maid, who provided housekeeping, several stable boys and a groundskeeper, and a man named Wally who helped with the administrative aspects of the business, including payroll and the details of our financial transactions. The original idea had been for Henry to take over that part of the business, but a few months into it, he'd asked to be released from what he called the

THE REBEL

prison of indoor work. We'd hired Wally after that. I was of the same mind, wishing to be outside training and caring for our horses. My father oversaw all the breeding himself, making sure to keep copious notes about the stallions and mares.

For lunch, I sat in my usual spot at the table. We always said a prayer first, asking the Lord to bless our meal and to say thanks. My father usually led the prayer, so I was surprised when he asked me to do the honors.

I bowed my head. "Lord, thank you for the gift of this meal. Please keep our loved ones safe during these hard times. Be with us as we prepare to fight for freedom. Amen."

Papa and I devoured our meal without saying much. Mother ate a few bites of the soup but then pushed her spoon around the bowl as if searching for buried treasure. Since we'd completed the enlistment process, she'd been quiet and withdrawn. She'd been appalled at my decision to join the marines, especially after I admitted that it was because the line was shorter. The twins had waited for a long time to join the army.

"I received notice already," I said. "I'm to report to training in Virginia in two weeks."

My mother's spoon clattered onto the table. "Two weeks. But that's not enough time to prepare."

"They want us trained quickly, Mama. There's urgency to get us on the ground fighting." I glanced at Papa. He stared into his empty bowl.

"Papa?" I wanted to ask him if he was all right and reassure him that I would be fine, but the words didn't come.

He nodded at me. "I'm glad to know what to expect. Takes the guessing work out of it."

"There will be opportunities for specialty training if I show any potential for certain things," I said.

Mama brightened. "Specialties. Ones that will keep you from the front lines."

"I'll do my best and see what happens."

81

"That's all we can ask of you," Papa said.

"There's something else." I sipped water to dampen my dry mouth. It suddenly felt as if cotton balls had been stuffed into the back of my throat. "Delphia has agreed to marry me before I leave."

My mother set her napkin down. Her eyes showed a little more hope than the moment before. "Have you asked her father yet?"

"Not yet but I'm planning on it," I said.

"Why so quick?" Papa asked. "This seems to have come out of nowhere."

"Not really," I said. "We've both felt this way for a long time. I've been patient, and she's finally come home. I don't want to wait until after I get home from the war. She and I want to be married before I ship out, in case anything happens to me over there."

"You're sure?" Papa asked. "Marriage is forever."

"I know. I can't believe she said yes."

Mama smiled and put her napkin back on her lap. "She *is* a remarkable girl. None better in my opinion. Like her mother."

"I agree," I said, going on to explain that she would continue to live at home with her parents until I returned. "At which point, we'll find a house of our own." I hadn't thought too much about where we would live. These things had a way of working themselves out.

"She's prepared to be the wife of a horse breeder?" Mama asked. "It's farm life. She might not be aware of all that it entails. Being a farmer's wife is not always easy."

"She'll have her own work, most likely." I explained about her desire to run the nightclub.

"The club?" Mama asked, sounding horrified. "A woman?"

"She is who she is, Mama, and I don't plan on trying to change her."

"Good idea," Papa said, eyes twinkling. "The secret to a good marriage is to accept the person as they are, not how you wish them to be."

"I wish for Delphia. That is all," I said.

"Then you have our blessing." Mama dabbed at her mouth. "Do you have a ring for her?"

"Not yet. I'll have to get us both wedding bands."

What followed were a series of questions from my mother about the wedding and reception. I explained about a church gathering and then just a small party with family and close friends at the Barnes home afterward. "Delphia wants something simple."

"Sensible," Mama said. "Especially given the current situation." She shook her head, looking happier than she had in days. "To think, I was once her mother's maid. America is a wonderful place where anything can happen."

We didn't say much after that, finishing the rest of the bread. Working outside made a man hungry. After the meal, I went upstairs to my room to bathe and change clothes. I left for the Barneses' place shortly thereafter with hope in my heart that he would also give us his blessing.

ARMED WITH NOTHING more than my respect for Lord Barnes, I headed to his home. The sky was milky. Snow would soon come. What would it be like where I was headed? I wondered. Would it be cold? Would there be snow? I'd not been out of the country before, journeying only as far as the East Coast for business transactions for our family business. Perhaps the marines would be an adventure.

Delphia came running out of the house when I arrived, wearing a pair of trousers and a sweater. Her hair was pulled back with a blue scarf. Other than red lipstick, she wore no makeup.

"I'm sorry for my appearance," Delphia said breathless and throwing herself into my arms. "I've been helping Mama sort through the attic. She's keeping herself busy and roped me into helping."

I kissed her lightly on the mouth. "You look beautiful. I like fresh-faced you."

"Good, because that's who you'll wake up to for the rest of your life."

"Speaking of which, I'm here to see your father." I smiled down at her. "This is your last chance to back out."

"I'll not be doing so. You're stuck with me now." She hugged herself around the waist, shivering. It was cold, and she didn't have a jacket on. "He's in the barn, spending time with the horses."

"Keeping busy, too?" I asked.

"I believe so."

"Wish me luck."

"You won't need it. He's ready for you."

"Get back inside. It's freezing out here." I kissed the end of her adorable nose and headed toward the barn.

Lord Barnes looked up from brushing one of his horses when I came in through the side door. "Well, there he is. The man who dares to take my last daughter away from me." His British accent was as strong as it had ever been, making him seem smart and elegant, like the nobleman he was, I supposed.

"Yes, sir." I stuck my hands in my pockets. In my nervousness, I'd forgotten my leather driving gloves, and my fingertips were cold. "I would very much like to marry Delphia, sir, and am asking for your blessing."

He patted the horse's neck before turning toward me, his eyes glassy. "This is the last time a young man will ever ask me this. Delphia's my last one—my baby. I would like to keep her here with us forever, but alas, I will have to let her go, too." He smiled, mischievously. "If not, given Delphia, I'll never hear the end of it if I don't let her have what she wants."

"Thank you, sir." I held out my hand and we shook.

He went back to brushing the horse, who neighed happily. "Your father took care of my very first horses. Did you know that?"

"Yes, I did, sir."

"We used to have only the sleighs back then. What fun we had—all those tinkling bells under a starry sky. I fell in love with Delphia's mother on one of those nights. From that moment on, I pledged to devote my life to her and her happiness. I'll expect you to do the same with my youngest daughter."

"You have my word." I flattened my hand in the air by my thigh to indicate how small we'd been when I first loved her. "Since we were this high, I've wanted nothing more than to give her whatever she wished for. I didn't know what it meant back then. I thought it was only a desire to keep her safe from harm on the playground or down at the creek. As it turned out, I was in love with her even back then. My entire world has always been Delphia. I don't expect that'll ever change until one of us goes up to meet the Lord."

"A long, long time from now." Lord Barnes set aside his brush and came closer to the door of the stall and put his hands on my shoulders. "You come back to her, do you understand me? You must do everything to stay alive."

"That's my intention, sir."

He sighed and dipped his chin. "All of you boys—our boys— it's hard to see you all walk into danger this way, but yet I can't help but be proud of how brave you all are. I'll wear out the knees of my trousers praying, I can assure you of that."

"I'll come back to her, sir. We all will. These women are the finest in the world. It's only right we come home to them."

"See that you do."

I nodded and headed away from him but then turned back

to say one last thing. "Sir, if I don't have another chance, I wanted to thank you for everything you did for my family. We'll never forget it."

"Your father's made that clear enough, young man, but thank you just the same. Truthfully, people make their own luck through hard work. Your father earned every bit of his success. There's no need for further thanks from either one of you."

I thanked him again, even though he'd just said not to, and made my way toward my car. I'd promised Delphia that I'd take her for a ride in our sleigh later. We'd just broken two colts who were now as docile as a couple of bunnies, and I wanted to show them off to her. I made a mental note to make sure they had bells around their necks. For old times' sake.

9

DELPHIA

We arrived at our special spot in the woods where my father had built a firepit and a picnic area in Jack's sleigh, pulled by two of his newly trained colts. I'd suggested we go out to our family park, and Jack had readily agreed. My father had created it in an area not far from the main house for family gatherings. Long picnic tables were built on a platform with an awning overhead so that we could enjoy it all year round. A large firepit made of river rock was situated about twenty yards from the structure. It had been a common meeting place for us when we were in high school.

As we pulled to a stop, we were surprised to see Beaumont and Bleu already there, sitting around the firepit.

Jack looked at me, laughing. "So much for our romantic evening."

"We don't have to stay long," I whispered.

"Kind of like old times, though?" Jack said, a sentimental hitch in his throat.

The boys and I had spent many nights here as teenagers, gossiping and teasing one another. Sometimes, if the mood was right, we'd talked of the future, our dreams, and aspirations.

They'd never made me feel ashamed about my ambitions for college and beyond, treating me as their equal. The boys were just as smart as I, but they didn't care about being the best the way I did. Maybe because they were men, they had the luxury to care less about their places in the world. I had to fight a little harder for everything than they did. Regardless, they'd always acted proud of me and teased me as much as they did one another, which was the highest of compliments.

"Do they know about us?" I asked quietly as Jack helped me from the sled.

He shrugged a little sheepishly. "I told them when we went to Denver to enlist. We had a lot of time to talk while waiting." He explained that at the recruitment center, they'd arrived to long lines of men waiting to enlist. They'd stood in line all morning but finally managed to fill out the necessary paperwork and receive their assignments to training camp. I'd not expected Jack to sign up with the marines. I didn't know what that meant exactly, other than it terrified me. He brushed off my concern, saying the line was a lot shorter.

The weather was cold but clear. We sat together on one of the four wide benches that surrounded the pit. Phillip had built them so the maximum number of people could sit around the fire. Jack had his arm tucked around my waist, holding me against his side. I'd have thought it would be strange, but it felt just right. As if we'd always been this way.

"We thought for a minute about joining the marines," Beaumont said. "The line was much shorter."

Bleu took a swig of booze from his flask before adding, "And here I thought we were early and more patriotic than the rest, but when we got there to see lines as long as the length of a football field, we could see we weren't as special as we thought."

We reminisced for a good thirty minutes, laughing until our sides hurt about the time Beaumont had accidentally left his parents' garden gate open only to find that bunnies had eaten every last leaf of lettuce and herbs of the spring crop. Fiona and Li had been out of town for a few days when we discovered the carnage. Instead of owning up to his mistake, he'd convinced us to transplant lettuce from Mama and Papa's garden. It seemed like a perfectly fine idea to our ten-year-old selves. In the middle of the night, we'd met to dig up the baby lettuces from our garden to plant in their plot. Unfortunately, we woke the next morning to nothing but dead lettuce and herbs. Our empty patch, after being robbed of its yields, had flummoxed the poor gardener who looked after our vegetable plots. He'd come into the kitchen, Lizzie told me later, and asked if he could have a nip of the cooking sherry because he was sure to be fired anyway and he might as well be drunk while it happened.

"He kept repeating over and over that a ghost had come and stolen all the lettuces," I said now. "The poor man."

"The moment she arrived home, our mother figured out exactly what we'd done," Bleu said. "I'd never seen her so mad."

"My mother was, too," I said, shuddering.

"Mine too," Jack said. "It was a shame we never had our birthday parties because of it."

That had been the agreed-upon punishment by our mothers. There were absolutely no eleventh year parties for the guilty. Leaving the gate open was one thing, my mother had said, but the botched cover-up job was another.

"Mama was most disappointed with the idea I would let the gardener take the fall, remember?" I shivered again, my former shame coming back to me. "I'm ashamed to say that never even occurred to me."

"Us either," Bleu said. "Our mother was mad about that too."

"She's gentle, until angry," Beaumont said, laughing.

"I have a gift for making my mother mad," I said. "Do you remember the time I interfered with James and Addie?"

"No, what did you do?" Bleu asked.

89

I recounted the story of my unwanted interference in Addie's love life. I'd been sixteen and thought I was helping them be together by getting Lena, James's fiancée, into trouble. That had not worked out. Instead, I was the one in trouble. Fortunately for all, Lena and her husband had moved here and now had two little boys. They were the happiest of couples and had fit right into our community. As it turned out, Lena wasn't a fox at all, only a scared young woman who felt she was without any choices about who she married or how she conducted her life. In further strangeness, she and Addie had become good friends, as had their husbands. "I still feel bad about it every time I see Lena in town."

"Yes, but that had a happy ending," Jack said encouragingly.

"I suppose you could say that about all our mistakes," Bleu said. "We learned from them—and carry those lessons into everything we do now."

"Some of us needed more lessons than others," I said, speaking of myself.

We talked for a few more minutes about other scrapes the four of us had gotten into. "Remember when Delphia had the bright idea to prove that fairies existed in our woods?" Beaumont asked.

"I forgot about that," Jack said, slapping his knee.

"I thought for sure we'd be eaten by wolves," Bleu said.

"We weren't in any real danger." I rolled my eyes. "Not really, anyway."

"You were always thinking of ways to get us all in trouble," Beaumont said. "Not that we fought you for long on any of your ideas."

"We usually thought they were fine ideas," Jack said. "How old were we during the fairy quest?"

"Nine," I said. "I remember it well."

That summer, I'd become obsessed with the idea that tiny fairies lived in trees near our house. It took some time, but I'd finally convinced the boys to join me in my quest to prove the theory true. "You all wanted to capture one to bring home and show all the doubters," I said. "That's how I convinced you."

No fairies had been found. We'd gotten very lost in the woods. Night fell and we decided to hunker down under the protection of a large tree to wait for the morning light before attempting to find our way out of what had suddenly become a maze.

The next morning, we woke to find that mosquitoes had bitten us wherever our bare skin had been exposed. I had the worst of it, as they'd found their way under my skirt. I'd refused to wear dresses for the rest of the summer. Not only did the bites leave me with ugly purple spots, I would wake from nightmares of the nasty little bugs feasting on my dead body. Even now, all these years later, I shivered at the thought of that night.

"I thought the mosquito bites were bad until I faced my mother and father," Bleu said. "My father had been up all night, pacing the floor. My mother's eyes were red and swollen from crying. I never felt so bad in my life. Well, except for the garden incident."

"We had way too many ideas for our own good," I said.

"Mostly the three of you," Jack said. "And I just went along."

"Bad mistake," Beaumont said, laughing.

We were quiet for a moment, all of us lost in our own memories. "We had some fun times, though, didn't we?" I asked.

"The best," Bleu said.

"We've missed you, Delphia," Beaumont said. "Although we've gotten in fewer scrapes."

"I'm sorry," I said. "Trouble just seemed to follow me wherever I went."

"And Jack," Bleu said. "He followed you wherever you went as well."

"He did?" I asked. "I don't remember it that way."

"I do," Jack said. "You've always had me wrapped around your finger."

"And now you're getting hitched," Bleu said.

"About time, if you ask me," Beaumont said. "I'll be able to finally collect my debt from my brother here."

"Bet?" I asked.

"Yeah, we had a wager about when you two would finally figure it out." Beaumont took a small flask from his pocket. "I said it would be shortly after you finally came home for good." He tilted his flask back to take a drink, then handed it to his brother.

"I'd said you'd come home after college and get engaged right after." Bleu gave his head a rueful shake. "I didn't predict you taking that job after you graduated."

"We thought then you might never come home," Beaumont said. "I'm glad we were wrong."

"I wanted to prove to myself that I could make my own way without my family's help." I declined the offer of the flask. Jack took it instead, the scent of alcohol strong as he tipped it up to take a sip.

"Yeah, I know. I was the same," Bleu said. "But here I am, back working for the family."

"There's nothing wrong with it," Jack said. "We're all blessed to be in families that look after their own."

The fire crackled and several logs collapsed, splintering into red-hot coals. My feet and legs were toasty from the heat.

"I never said this to you before," Bleu said, his attention on me. "But I figure I might as well, you know, in case anything happens to me over there."

"Don't say it." I held up my hand. "I can't hear any talk of that."

"Well, I'm going to say this anyway." Bleu pushed a lock of his brown hair away from his forehead. "I want to thank you for

taking us in the way you did when we first got here. Both of you
—just folded us right in as if we'd always been here."

"Yeah. We were so scared to come here," Beaumont said.
"When we got to Colorado, we discovered that not only did we
get adopted by two caring people, but we were embraced by
their family and friends, too. Even though we couldn't understand half of what you said for the first year we lived here."

"We couldn't understand you, either," Jack said. "It didn't
seem to make that much difference. We all knew how to hike
through these woods together. Language out here comes from
the critters and birds, the crunch of leaves in the fall, the smell
of pines on a summer night."

My heart ached with love for my poetic horseman. "The
scent of wildflowers in spring."

"Or roses in August," Jack said. "That's the language of
Emerson Pass. We have it imprinted in our hearts."

"The words of an artist, right there," Bleu said.

Jack laughed. "Not really. I love this place, though. It's in my
blood."

"For me too," Beaumont said. "After the dirty streets where
we'd lived after our real mother died, this place seemed like
heaven. I can remember looking at the stars at night that first
summer and thinking—where am I and how did I get here?"

"We never looked back," Bleu said. "From the minute we
arrived, we knew this was home."

"It is *our* home," I said softly. "And when you boys get back,
it'll still be here waiting for you. As will I."

"And we'll sit around this fire just like we are now," Jack said,
pulling me closer. "You keep these home fires burning, Delphia."

"I will." I buried my face against the collar of his jacket,
taking in the scent of spice and pine needles that always accompanied him. *Keep these memories close*, I told myself. *They will be
all I have until these boys all come home.*

TESS THOMPSON

JACK and I sat together on my parents' back porch. He'd gotten his instructions. He was to report to basic training in two weeks' time. We'd have a week together as a married couple before he left, then after that, he would be sent to boot camp.

Between the sleigh ride and time with the twins, I'd not had a chance to ask him about the talk with my father, so he filled me in now, telling me all the details. He knew I liked to know every single word that was said.

"So, in conclusion, he gave me his consent," Jack said.

"I knew he would." I turned away from him to gaze back out at the yard. Snow fell in fat flakes, beautiful in the lamplight.

"Something occurred to me today," Jack said. "I have to leave a few days before Christmas."

"I know. It's sad but can't be helped. We must be brave. I'll send your present with you so you'll have a part of me with you on Christmas Day."

"I want all of you with me."

"I want that too. God willing, this war will be over soon."

"God willing."

"I should go," Jack said. "I promised Papa I'd be back as soon as I could."

I gritted my teeth to keep from tearing up. "Be sure to tell your father that Cym and I could help. She loves horses. We can arrange to be available if he needs us."

"What about the nightclub?"

"Yes, that." I paused, chewing on the inside of my lip. "We might close it while the war's on. Use the space for the war effort. That's what my mother wants, and we want to give that to her. We can open up again when all this is over. For now, we can use it for good."

His eyes shone with so much love it almost brought tears to

94

my eyes. "I think that sounds great. I'll tell my dad about you and Cym."

We kissed goodnight before I walked him around the house and watched as he got into his car. We'd dropped the horses and sleigh off at his house before he took me home in the car. He waved to me and I waved back, then stepped into the warmth of the house.

As I passed by the sitting room, I heard a noise. Peeping in, I saw that it was Mama, sitting in the dark with the only light from the fireplace. She had a hanky up to her mouth, silently sobbing. Obviously, she'd not heard me come in.

"Mama, are you all right?"

She jumped, clearly startled, and wiped her eyes. "I'm fine."

She was certainly not fine. I raced across the room toward her while shrugging out of my coat. Falling at her feet, I placed both hands on her knees. She wore her dressing gown and robe. Even with the silk covering, I could feel how cold her legs were underneath. How long had she been sitting here in the dark?

"Mama, what is it?"

"Nothing to worry over. Go on up to bed." She unfolded her hanky and spread it over her lap, as if that proved that all was well.

"Mama, did something happen? Or are you just sad?"

"I'm just sad." She patted the cushion next to her. "If you won't go upstairs, at least you can sit next to me and hold my hand."

I did as she asked, taking her small, cold hand into mine.

"I stupidly thought I wouldn't have to go through this again," Mama said. "Sending all my boys and my grandsons off to war, not being able to breathe from worry. Jack, too, who will now be family. I don't know if I'm strong enough to withstand it all."

"You are, Mama. You're the strongest person I know. I'll be here, too. We will try to bear it together."

"Oh, you are a darling girl, my Delphia. I'm glad you're home."

"Me too."

She turned to look into my eyes. "And you're truly sure about Jack?"

"I know it seems fast but really, we've been leading up to this since we were in high school. I love him, Mama."

She sighed. "I wish you could have a proper dress like the other girls had."

"Do you know what? I really don't care about the dress. I just want Jack."

"Ah, then, you know it's real."

We talked about the wedding and my plan to stay here at the house while Jack was away as the fire turned to embers. "Your father and I want to give you the empty cottage as a wedding gift. It needs a lot of work, but it'll give you something to work on while he's gone. Phillip will help, I'm sure." The cottage she referred to was about a mile from here. No one had lived in it since Clive and Annabelle had first wed. After her wedding gown business became popular, they'd built a big house down by the river.

"Mama, really? I'm so happy."

"It'll be nice to have something to focus on while he's gone." She paused, plucking at the buttons of her robe. "Are you aware of what happens on the wedding night?"

I flushed probably every shade of pink in succession. "Yes, Mama. I'm aware. After experiencing kissing, I have to say I'm looking forward to it."

"It's a special, wonderful thing when it's between two people who love each other. Two *married* people, I should add."

"Of course, Mama. My virtue is intact."

"I'm glad, dear one. You won't regret saving it all for Jack." She folded her hanky back into a square. "Did I ever tell you about the first time I met Merry? I shocked her quite a bit by telling her I was perfectly capable of dressing myself. She was young like me and hadn't experienced much. In addition, she'd been trained by Jasper, who was such a stickler for doing everything the proper way. I shocked her. She just stared at me helpless, worried she would get in trouble if she went downstairs without helping me. But we got through it. I adjusted to being a lady of a house instead of a poor, hungry waif. Then she became the lady of her own house and had those darling boys. Now here we are. The marriage of our children. America *is* a wonderful place. I know we must defend it to the death but still, selfishly, I don't want it to be my boys."

"I know, Mama. Me either."

Papa appeared in his striped pajamas, silver hair standing on end. "What are you two doing up? It's past midnight."

"I couldn't sleep," Mama said.

"And I only just got home from being with Jack and the twins. We were out at the firepit."

He nodded, smiling indulgently. "Well, I cannot sleep when my wife's not next to me. So either we all have a cup of tea with a little whiskey or we go upstairs."

Mama shook her head, smiling at my father. He could always cheer her. "Goodness, Alexander. Tea and whiskey. Whoever heard of such a thing. I'll come upstairs."

We all went up the stairs together, pausing to hug before I went farther down the hallway to my bedroom. *The house is too quiet*, I thought. *Where did they all go?*

They grew up, a voice whispered in my head. *Just as you will.* Time rolls on, waiting for no one, whether we're ready or not.

10

DELPHIA

We were married on a snowy Saturday one week after our first official date. My family was there, loud and weepy and delighted for us. Although I had disappointed my aunt Annabelle with the news of my hasty wedding, she had whipped up an attractive white suit and pillbox hat with a white net over the front. The ceremony was held at the church with our pastor conducting the exchange of vows. Afterward, we returned to the main house for champagne and one of Lizzie's feasts. There were toasts and funny stories told about both of us, and everyone put on a happy face. However, underneath all the joy for our union, a dark kernel of dread for what was to come lived inside us.

Everyone had their orders by then. Our only happy news was that Flynn had failed the physical examination because of an old skiing injury that had broken his leg in two places. Apparently, they hadn't healed properly, most likely because he hadn't stayed off them long enough. So we would have Flynn at home. However, Addie had pulled me aside the day before the wedding to tell me that James was enlisting. "He can't watch as the rest of them go off to fight," she said tearfully.

James, with his big heart and sense of loyalty, had not been able to see any other way but to do his part. Although Addie understood, it didn't make the idea of his absence any easier. He would be sent to boot camp like the younger men, but Papa said he thought they'd find a clerical position where good writing skills were needed. This made Addie feel a little more confident that her husband would return to her in one piece.

Theo, who would leave in several weeks, had been assigned a position in a field hospital in France, treating the newly wounded before transferring them to convalescent care where they would either be sent back to fight or discharged to go home.

That left Bleu, Beaumont, and Jack. They were to report to basic training at the end of next week. It would take several days to get to Virginia on the train, leaving us four days for our honeymoon in Denver. I would send him on his way from there before returning to Emerson Pass.

But we had tonight to be together. We'd decided to spend our wedding night at the newly opened Emerson Pass Inn. What had once been a boardinghouse had been purchased by a wealthy widow and remodeled into an upscale inn. The hostess winked at me when she opened the door to the room and mentioned she saved it for newlyweds. Although cold and a little drafty, it was quaint and pretty with a metal-frame bed and a white quilt. An easy chair in the corner and a small desk made up the rest of the room. Nowhere to hide, I thought, as I gazed around the room where I would spend the first night of my married life.

I left Jack in the room while I stole away to put on my night-gown. After I'd undressed, I stood shivering in the bathroom, gazing at my reflection. My wedding night. *Don't be afraid*, I told myself. *This is Jack. He's the one you've wanted forever.*

I unpinned my hair from its usual tidy style so that it brushed the tops of my shoulders. Using cold cream, I wiped away my wedding-day makeup. My skin seemed pale without the help of rouge and my lips blue.

The silk dressing gown and matching robe had been made by Josephine especially for the occasion, both of which clung to my hip bones and stomach. The last few weeks had been busy and nerve-racking, thus the weight I'd like to have added to my small frame had not come to pass. I shivered, suddenly terrified to go out to the room where my new husband waited. *It's only Jack*, I reminded myself. My best friend. The man who knew me better than anyone else and liked me anyway. Loved me, actually.

I flashed upon the moment of our vows from earlier. We'd been blessed with sunshine that had streamed through the windows of the church in a thin wintry light. Jack wore his best suit and tie and looked so handsome my knees had weakened at the sight of him. We'd promised to love and cherish each other and exchanged rings before kissing.

I'd looked into Jack's eyes after the kiss and before we made our way back down the aisle of our small church. A peace had washed over me. This was right. Jack and I were meant for each other, and God had blessed us with the gift of true love.

Now, I drew in a deep breath and went out to meet my husband. He was sitting in the easy chair wearing only trousers and a white undershirt, the straps of his suspenders hanging over his hips. The muscles in his arms and torso strained again the thin cotton of his tee as he stood to greet me.

"Hello, beautiful." He took both my hands and kissed each of them before drawing me close. "You're trembling. Are you cold?"

"A little. Mostly nervous."

"Me too, if you want to know the truth," he said. "This is strange, isn't it?"

"You mean me and you?"

"No, not that. Never that. I just meant being here—on our wedding night. It's a little unbelievable, almost like a dream."

"Yes, a wonderful dream." I gazed up at him, noticing the shadow of whiskers on his chin, and brushed my thumb against the stiff bristles.

"Come to bed, Mrs. Depaul?"

I couldn't trust myself to speak, so simply nodded and let him lead the way.

THE MORNING AFTER, we left for a three-night stay in Denver. Thankfully, Jack had said his goodbyes to everyone at the wedding reception and we were able to board the train to Denver without any more tears. The next four days were the best of my life. We did not spend much time exploring the city. Indeed, mostly we stayed in bed learning the ways of love and each other. I'd not imagined anything could feel as good as being with Jack. If I thought I was in love with him before, I was even more so now. The idea of parting from him seemed unbearable.

Yet the end of our time together inevitably arrived, as it does. The morning we were to say goodbye, I woke up with a pit in my stomach. I rolled over to get one last look at my husband. He was still asleep, curled on his side, his dark lashes splayed against his high cheekbones and the muscles of his face relaxed. Would I ever tire of watching him breathe or eat or sleep or talk? I didn't think it was possible.

He woke a few minutes later to find me still watching him. He blinked and twitched slightly before breaking into a smile. "I'm sorry. Did I scare you?" I asked, laughing.

"Nah. I was dreaming of the river in summer, swimming with you. You were wearing that blue suit with the white polka dots. I love that one." He reached out to pull me to him, burying his face in my hair. "How can it be time to say goodbye already?"

"I don't know. It went too fast." My throat hitched. "Please, come back to me."

"I will, my love. I will."

Later, as I stood on the platform in the Denver station, I couldn't help but cry as he walked up the steps to his seat. All around me were similar scenes. Mothers and sisters and wives weeping as the men they loved boarded a train for a journey into the unknown.

When he got to his seat, he opened the window and leaned out. I ran to him and took his hand that draped from the window frame. "I love you. Don't forget how much," I said.

"I won't forget. You won't forget me either, will you? Or how much I love and adore you?"

The train was starting to pull out of the station. I ran alongside until it was impossible to do so and then stopped, waving and blowing kisses until I could no longer see him. Then I turned away and made my way through the crowds of people on the platform and inside the station itself until I was out to the street. Snow fell, more shards of ice than soft flakes that stung my cheeks. I buttoned the top of my coat and stood there, lost for a moment and uncertain what to do next. My train to Emerson Pass wouldn't leave for hours yet. I had nothing but time. Too much time. I just wanted to go home.

I was about to start up with the crying again when out of the corner of my eye, I saw a clump of women headed my way. What a sight they were! My sisters. All of them. Addie and Cym, arms linked, were in the lead. Addie wore a blue coat I'd never seen before, and Cym wore her red wool and black heels that showed off her muscular calves. Behind them were Fiona and Josephine. Fiona's face was the color of her light gray trench coat and her eyes were red and puffy. She was more of a wreck than I. Josephine, tall and steady, reached me first, pulling me into a hug. Following slightly behind was my mother. She looked so small and frightened, I wanted to hug her, forgetting for a moment my own angst out of concern for her.

"We're here to take you to tea," Jo said. "And then home."

But how was it possible they were all here? "Addie? Why are you here? Shouldn't you be home with James before he has to go?"

"He left yesterday," she said, bottom lip quivering. "I came with him to Denver and saw him off this morning. We didn't want to disturb you on your honeymoon, so I didn't tell you."

"I sent the twins off yesterday," Fiona said. "Josephine thought it would be a good distraction if we all came to fetch you and Addie and bring you home with us."

"But not before a nice tea and dinner out," Cym said. "Fiona has a friend performing at a club tonight. We thought we could spend the night together and then all go back in the morning."

"Mama got us rooms at the Strater Hotel," Jo said. "And if we can hustle, we can get there by the time they serve tea."

My eyes welled with gratitude. "I'm so glad to see you all. You've no idea."

"I do," Addie said softly. "They surprised me as well. It was so hard, wasn't it?"

"Yes, very much so."

The six of us made our way down the street, hailing a cab to take us to the Strater. As I snuggled into the back seat between Addie and Cym, I remembered what it was like to be the littlest sister, taken such good care of all my life. How lucky I was. I must remember that always.

11

JACK

I thrived at basic training. Physically, learning to be a marine was challenging but not impossible. I'd been working hard all my life on the farm. In most ways, I was more prepared than others for the strenuous nature of our instructions. The discipline they required of us in our daily habits felt as familiar as putting on a favorite old jacket. I loved the neatness and precision required to be a marine. While some of my peers struggled with authority or the physical demands, I welcomed both. The very nature of the brutal training bonded the men quickly. We learned that the most important thing was to work as a team and to take care of one another.

Thus, by the time my assignment came, I felt ready. On the last day before I shipped out, I wrote to my wife.

Dearest Delphia,

I'm being shipped off to New York and then to Northern Ireland. After that, we're going to a secret location in the South Pacific. I can't tell you more than that. Even if I tried, they would blot it out in the letter. It's important we keep our secrets from the enemy.

All in all, I'm doing well, feeling strong and fit. I'd be lying if I didn't say the immediate future is frightening. You and I both know

I'm heading into danger. However, I'll do my best to be smart in every-thing I do. I want nothing more than to come home to you when this is all over and properly begin our lives together.

I was thinking this morning of our wedding day. You looked beau-tiful coming down that aisle on your father's arm. I'll keep that image close in the days to come.

Write when you can and tell me how everything's going back home. I'm terribly homesick for all of you and the Colorado sky. Be well, my darling.

Love,

Jack

As I'd said in the letter, I was shipped out of New York to Northern Ireland. What I couldn't say to Delphia was that from there we were then sent to Guadalcanal in the Solomon Islands. I'd never heard of the place but soon knew more about it than I'd ever have wished upon myself or the other men. Sticky and full of bugs, it was like walking around in the mist of a hot shower while waving away bloodthirsty mosquitoes.

Under the code name Operation Watchtower, we were the first to begin a major land offensive in our fight with Japan. Located north of Australia, the Solomon Islands had been occu-pied by Japanese defenders since May. Fortunately for us, they were mostly construction troops, and we managed to surprise them. They gave us no trouble, surrendering power almost immediately, allowing us to seize the southern islands. We then took over a partial landing strip we called Henderson Field, meant to be a defense perimeter.

I wasn't privy to strategy, but we quickly understood that we had few supplies or resources. Food was scarce. We had no maps to guide us. The mosquitoes were thick and hungry. Heat and humidity made it seem as if we were in a large steam bath. Patrolling the area through water and muck became our primary job. Amongst the men, we called it Operation Shoe-string because it became obvious from the beginning that it was not well-funded and there weren't enough marines. They didn't tell us much, but we knew the decision to send us to the Solomon Islands had been made hastily, mostly to take advantage of the recent sinking of four out of the six Japanese aircraft carriers in the area, which gave us the lead in the initiative.

Our defense of a small rise south of Henderson Field, Edson's Ridge, was our primary concern. If we could keep it from the Japanese, we could station aircraft on the island. The Japanese would have to fly all the way from the island of Rabaul, five hundred and some miles away.

I had no idea if my letters would reach home, but I wrote them anyway. The thought of my folks and Delphia not knowing where I was or that I was well made me nearly insane with worry. In my letters, I was careful to sound upbeat and as though all was well. If they had any idea of what it was really like over here, they wouldn't be able to sleep a wink.

Dearest Delphia,

My darling wife, I've arrived to my destination. They've asked that we not disclose to our loved ones any details of where we are. You might find this letter blacked out, so don't be concerned if it is. We're careful to keep secrets from our enemies. After weeks in Northern Ireland, we were sent to our current destination in preparation for battle. Thus far, the conditions are fine. They have us situated in a luxury ship! Tonight they even played a movie for us. I'm assuming it was to keep our minds off the upcoming battles. All in all, things are fine. We haven't seen any fighting yet. The enemy in this particular place surrendered without any fighting.

I think of you constantly and cannot wait until I return to you and our life in Emerson Pass. When I close my eyes at night, it is only you I dream of.

All my love,

Jack

The next day, I woke to disheartening news. Admiral Frank Jack Fletcher, our task force commander, had abandoned us, feeling his ships were too vulnerable to attacks from our enemy. He'd ordered the fleet to leave us. It took me a moment to understand that we were not only without their help in the fight but that we were also left without supplies.

We went about our usual tasks that day, but the easy camaraderie and joking had been dampened by the truth of our situation. That night, Japan cruisers arrived and sank four of our heavy cruisers off Savo Island. We were alone and without protection. The navy had left us out here to die.

The rest of August proved to be rough for us. We had little food, living on rice we found on the island and dried fish. The morale of the boys was low, and we complained a lot about hunger and the vicious mosquitoes. I stopped writing letters home, knowing there was no way to send them.

We hung on for the rest of the month with constant attacks. The night of September 12th, attacks came from all sides.

I was sent out with several others to scope out the sea from up on the hill. It would be my last mission.

12

DELPHIA

I didn't hear from Jack after his letter written in early August. The days inched along, and I was sick with worry. My father suggested I put my nervous energy to good use and begin to remodel the cottage so that it was ready for Jack when he came home. One day when I was morosely flopping around the kitchen, Lizzie offered to teach me to cook. "Your man deserves a home-cooked meal when he comes home from this awful war."

"Me? Cook? I don't know, Lizzie. It doesn't sound like me."

She laughed and pulled me into a hug. "I know, love, but think of how happy it will make Jack if his wife knows how to cook a decent meal."

I had to laugh, imagining his face if I were to present a bowl of homemade chicken soup. "He won't recognize me."

"Not to worry about that," Lizzie said. "He'll have a full stomach in addition to his beautiful wife and know he's home."

For the next month, I spent every morning with Lizzie learning how to make breads and stews and pies. I found pies particularly challenging. My dough would never roll out properly. But after a few weeks, even my crust started to cooperate.

In preparation for Thanksgiving, Lizzie spent a whole morning on sauces and gravies. Mine were all lumpy at first, but soon I developed the proper techniques. To my surprise, I enjoyed myself. Partly, it was the company of Lizzie and often my mother, too. We chatted while we cooked, reminiscing or talking of the future, making the mornings fly by.

With my sisters, we organized war efforts for the Red Cross, including knitting socks and gloves, putting together care packages, and whatever else needed to be done. As a community, we thought only of the war. Of our young men who bravely served and those who loved them. In the evenings, we were all glued to the radio, hoping for news that would reassure us that the war would soon be over. We got no such word, however.

Still, by keeping busy, I was able to continue on even though the letters from Jack had stopped arriving. I was down on my knees in prayer every night before climbing into bed exhausted from my work.

Although they were calling up men Phillip's age, he'd been deemed unfit because of the damage the Spanish flu had done to his lungs. James was working for one of the war newspapers, writing stories for the troops from a base in England. Theo was in France, running an army hospital near the front lines. The twins had been sent to Northern Africa at the beginning of the war and were there now, as far as we knew, but we hadn't heard much from either of them. Henry, having joined the navy, was on a ship somewhere in the South Pacific. Neither Lillian nor his parents got many letters from him, but they knew he was alive.

In addition to work, I'd spent time getting the cottage ready for Jack's return. With Phillip's help, we'd repainted and put in new kitchen appliances. The plumbing had been modernized. Phillip had made us a gorgeous dining room table and chairs. Mama and I had spent a few days in Denver picking out rugs and furniture. We'd just finished the final touches. I'd decided I would not move in until Jack came home to me. He would come home, I assured myself over and over as I made improvements to the decor and planned out a garden to plant next spring.

Phillip taught me how to sand wood until it was as smooth as silk, which I found comforting. There was something about a small movement done again and again that soothed my worries.

One day in late October of 1942, while I was at home knitting socks with my mother, the doorbell rang. We had a telegram from Jack.

Injured and being sent home. Expect me home sometime in December. Details forthcoming. Stop

That was all. I stood staring down at the simple words on that paper. Mama came to stand beside me, and I gave it to her with my shaking hand.

"What does it mean?" I asked, as if she would know.

"I don't know, darling, other than he's coming home."

I nearly fainted with relief. My husband was alive. But in what state? How injured was he? From what we heard, the injury must be dire or they'd have sent him back to fight.

I held on to Mama, my legs wobbly underneath me. Papa came out of his study and Mama handed him the telegram.

"It will be all right," Papa said, gathering me into an embrace. "He's alive. Whatever's happened, he's coming home."

I waited anxiously, hoping for a letter from Jack with more explanation, but none came. One evening about a week before Thanksgiving, our telephone rang. My heart leaped into my throat. I knew it was him. Jasper's heels on the hardwoods clicked as he went to answer the call as I rushed into the hallway. Jasper held out the receiver to me. "It's Jack."

"Hello, Jack?" I was breathless and dizzy, nerves making my stomach churn. "Are you really coming home?"

"Yes, as soon as I'm well enough to travel. I'm at a hospital in England. They told me today they think I'll be home by the middle of December."

"That's only weeks away. I can't believe it. You'll be home for Christmas."

"Delphia, you need to listen to me." His voice sounded strangled and dry. "I'm so sorry."

"What is it?" I gripped the edge of the hallway table and held my breath.

"I lost my right leg. I'd have died if they hadn't amputated it. Just above the kneecap."

"Oh, Jack." How could it be? My strong, proud husband without a limb? It was impossible. I shuddered, and dots danced before my eyes. Shaking and damp with fear, I thought I might be sick. Mama and Papa came to stand next to me, propping me up. "How did it happen?"

"A grenade. Went off next to me and ripped up my leg."

I must say the right thing, I thought. *He must understand how steadfast my love is for him.* "You're alive. That's all I care about."

"I'm sorry," he said again. "I did my best, but I'm coming home to you a fraction of the man I was."

"It doesn't matter. You're coming home. Whatever it is, we'll work through it together."

"Yeah, well, we'll see how you feel when I get there." The line went dead. He'd hung up on me? Just like that? I stared at the phone, unable to move.

"He…he's not there…he didn't say goodbye or the line went dead. I don't know. He sounded like a stranger." I felt like I was floating, disengaged from my body. "Like a different man." *Strangled* not *stranger.* Defeated and empty. And angry. Oh God, my poor Jack. He'd always prided himself on his toughness and athleticism.

"Darling, what's happened to him?" Mama asked, her face scrunched up in concern. She took the phone receiver from my hand and placed it back onto the base.

"He lost his right leg just above the knee. A grenade. They had to amputate." I said all this woodenly. Perhaps I was in shock. I don't know. I couldn't think straight, the buzzing between my ears nearly deafening.

Mama's face drained of color. A blue vein throbbed in the middle of her forehead.

My legs wobbled again and the black dots returned, swimming before me. "I feel faint," I whispered.

Papa scooped me up and took me into the sitting room and laid me on one of the sofas. Jasper said he would fetch tea. "Lizzie will want to know," he said almost to himself.

I sat between my parents, shaking and cold. "Addie. Where's Addie?" I asked, my voice breaking. "I need her."

"She's at home," Mama said. "I'll call her. She'll come right away, sweetheart."

"Yes, please." I needed to see Addie's face, to cling to her goodness.

My father took one of my hands. "Let's pray."

I nodded, numb. Mama took my other hand.

"Dear Lord, please stay with Jack as he recovers and subsequently is sent home. We ask that you restore his health and spirit. Thank you for sparing him." My father, who was a champion prayer, faltered, ending with a simple, "Amen."

"I just want him home," I said, crying. "I don't care about his leg." I didn't care, but I knew he would. A dread seeped in, crumpling me. What if he shut me out? He would be proud, perhaps too proud to be vulnerable and appear weak to the woman he loved. We'd had such little intimate time together as man and wife. Would this make him want to hide from me?

"We need to call Merry and Harley," Mama said. "They'll want to know."

I blinked, focusing on her face. Her color had not returned. She seemed as shaken as I. "I should call over there."

"Yes, they'll need our support," Mama said.

Papa brought over the phone we kept on Mama's desk, its long cord stretching just far enough. I dialed the Depauls' number. Merry picked up right away. "It's Delphia," I said. "Did you hear from Jack?"

"No, did he call?" She sounded as if she'd run a mile to get to the phone. He'd sent the telegram to me, and I'd given the good news to his parents. Now I would have to give the bad news.

"Yes, I just talked to him. He'll be home in December."

"Oh, thank the good Lord." I heard her tell the news to Harley, who must have been standing close.

"Merry, but there's more...he's..." I gulped in air. My head throbbed. I glanced at my father, who gave me an encouraging nod. "They had to amputate his right leg above the knee. A grenade exploded near him."

"Oh. Oh, I see," she said, quietly. The phone became muffled. I could not make out what Merry said to Harley.

Seconds later, he came on the line. "How did he sound?"

I glanced at my mother. She nodded, as if she had heard the question and was giving me permission to answer. "He didn't sound good. Not like himself."

"Well, that's to be expected," Harley said. "Don't worry. You'll cheer him up the minute he sees your pretty face. You two can get on with life and forget about this horrible war."

I doubted it would be as simple as that, but I thanked him anyway. His overly hopeful voice told me he was as shaken as I. His sense of protecting his family took precedence over his own fear, I supposed.

I hung up the phone and turned back to my parents. "What do I do now?"

"This is going to test your character and your union," Mama said. "But you can do it. You've always been able to do what God's required of you."

Was that true? It seemed to me that my life had always been easy. I'd gotten just what I wanted at every turn, even when I didn't deserve it. Was I strong enough to get through this? And pull Jack along with me?

MY PARENTS and I went out to see the Depauls later that evening, bringing one of Lizzie's pumpkin pies with us. Merry, who had obviously been crying, met us at the door. She had baby Jay on her hip. He squealed when he saw it was me. I'd been spending quite a bit of time here with him and Lillian, hoping to keep her mind off worrying with our visits while Jay played at our feet. I was grateful that Lillian had decided to remain with Merry and Harley instead of going to Denver. After her initial outburst, she'd come to her senses. If she hadn't, poor Merry would have been bereft without her grandson to dote upon.

Jay reached for me and I took him into my arms, kissing his fat cheeks. It hurt to think of how much Henry was missing of his son's childhood. All this sacrifice, I thought. Was it truly worth it? The number of casualties had been in the news. More and more loss of life every day.

Papa excused himself to go out to the barn to see Harley, leaving Mama and me with Merry and Lillian.

"Should we have some of this pie now?" Merry asked listlessly. I doubted she'd eaten since my phone call earlier.

"I'm not hungry," Mama said. "Save it for after your supper. We can't stay long anyway."

"Thank you for coming out," Merry said. "It's sweet of you."

"Let's leave the young ones here to chat and go talk in the kitchen." Mama linked arms with Merry, and they headed out of the room. Lillian, Jay, and I went into the cozy sitting room. A roaring fire blazed in the hearth. Temperatures had dropped below freezing just a few days before, and tonight it smelled as if it would snow.

"Are you holding up all right?" Lillian asked.

"I'm in shock, I think."

"I feel terrible about Jack," Lillian said. "I can't think of anything else. He and Henry are proud men. I don't know how he'll do."

I nodded, too sad to say out loud how much I agreed. Despite the tension between Henry and Jack before he left, the brothers were close. "I wish Henry was here," I said. "Jack will need him."

"As do I," Lillian said. "How will we make it through all of this? Some days I don't think I'm strong enough."

"You are. We both are."

We sat watching Jay play with his toy trucks. He'd added a new one to his collection, I noticed. Small and innocent, he had no idea what the adults in his life were going through. Thank goodness for that, at least.

"You'll be all right," Lillian said. "Jack's coming home."

"That's all I care about. I told him as much, but he didn't respond. Not really, anyway. After all these months, I thought he'd be happy to talk to me. Am I only thinking of myself? Do I sound awful?"

"Not at all. I would feel the same way, I'm sure." For the first time, I noticed that Lillian seemed dressed up for an ordinary weekday, in a light brown skirt and jacket over a silky blouse. "Were you out today?" I asked. "You look nice."

"Yes, well, I was at a job interview. I'm applying for a secretary position with the lawyer, Mr. Stocking. His secretary went to war."

"Do you want to work? What about Jay?"

"To be completely honest, we need the money. The bills haven't stopped just because Henry's gone. I thought I could put my typing skills to good use."

"You'll like it. Working has kept my mind off things. A little, anyway."

"Merry's offered to keep Jay for me. I think she wants to have more time with him anyway, so hopefully, it will work out for both of us."

"It seems all of us here at home are filling in for the men who are gone," I said. "Louisa told me yesterday that she's started helping Dr. Neal at the clinic. He said it didn't matter that she didn't have formal nursing training. She's been trailing along after Theo all these years. Any time she doesn't know something, she looks it up in the medical manuals."

"Gad, I hope she doesn't kill anyone."

This made us both giggle. "I'm sure she won't."

Lillian's face grew thoughtful as she reached for her cup of tea. "I was hoping to have another baby by now. We didn't want to wait too long to give Jay a sister or brother. Sometimes, when I'm feeling really low, I wonder if Henry will come back to us. Will it just be Jay and me forever?"

"We can't think that way."

"But we do," Lillian said.

That, indeed, was the truth.

A FEW DAYS LATER, I received a letter. I opened it with shaking hands and read it quickly.

Dear Mrs. Depaul,

I'm writing to you from a convalescent home in England where your husband is recovering from the amputation of his right leg. I've spent quite a bit of time with your husband during his recovery. His leg has healed nicely. However, his mental state is not good. He's depressed and despondent, refusing to do his exercises and eating very little. In the night, we hear him cry out from his dreams.

I thought it was best to write and tell you what to expect upon his return. He will need time and loving care to recover from such a life-altering event. Men in his situation and of his nature have a particularly hard time accepting help.

Practically speaking, I have a few suggestions. If it is possible, installing a shower that he can walk into would be very helpful. With his crutches, it will be hard to maneuver steps into a tub. We're spending time teaching him to use his crutches for stairs, and he's done well. As you know, he has many physical gifts, which have not been extinguished by the unfortunate amputation. He does not yet realize his resilience and strength, but I have no doubt that support from his family and being home with his loved ones will be the best medicine.

We've prepared a prosthetic for him, but I'll be the first to admit they need improvement. They're often ill-fitting, which can cause pain. Furthermore, they tend to cause blisters if worn too long. At this point, his wound is not ready for any pressure. Once the incisions have healed, the prosthetic will be very useful to him. Until then, he has crutches.

My other advice is to treat him as you always have. Do not do too much for him. He is perfectly capable of living a close to normal life, but you must give it time.

I wish you the best. I'll be praying for Jack and all who love him.

Sincerely,

Nurse Mary Forbes

By the time I'd finished, tears were rolling down my cheeks. How kind of her to write to me. She'd given me a great gift. The knowledge of what to expect. It was all I could cling to for now.

13

JACK

My leg ached. That was the darnedest thing. Nothing but space where it used to be, and yet I could feel pain as if my leg were still intact. Never mind all of that, I told myself, as I leaned a cheek against the cold window of the train car. We were pulling into the Emerson Pass station. I glanced out at the platform. Snow was falling. A light dusting covered the ground.

There she was. Delphia. Standing with my parents. God, she looked beautiful, wearing her blue wool coat and a winter hat that came down low over her forehead. Her cheeks were pink from the frigid weather, and she had her arms wrapped around herself. She was cold and possibly frightened to see me. Was she wondering if I was an ugly monster now? I was. My stump was pink and shiny and hideous. I could never show it to her. I wouldn't be able to stand the look of repulsion in her eyes.

How was I going to be married to the prettiest girl in town and pretend that I hadn't changed into something repulsive? How could I act as though everything was fine when my life was ruined? I wouldn't even be able to ride a horse. Plus, I'd grown weak in the hospital. I'd already been thin as a rail when I was shipped to England for surgery and convalescent time. Lying around for a month hadn't helped. That and I had no appetite. Ironic, since I'd been nothing but hungry since I'd left home.

I grabbed my blasted crutches and gingerly rose from my seat, then pulled my knapsack over my shoulder. The woman sitting opposite me averted her eyes. Staring at me, I thought. I'd best get used to it. This was my life now. She was curious, wondering what it looked like under my tied-up pant leg. I'd been lost in thought since getting on the train in Denver. Had she been staring at my leg the entire time?

"Thank you for serving our country and keeping us from harm," she said.

I looked up to see a pair of kind eyes on me. "Not really, ma'am, but thank you." She looked familiar. Who was she? Ah, yes, Theo and Dr. Neal's nurse. What was her name?

"I'm Dr. Neal's nurse. Mrs. O'Reilly. Mrs. Barnes told me you were to arrive home soon. How are you holding up? You've been very brave, I'm sure."

"Thank you, ma'am." Not brave. Not really.

"Come by and see Dr. Neal if you have any troubles. Or if you need anything at all during this adjustment period. Theo will be after me when he gets home if we don't take good care of you."

"Yeah, sure." Take care of me? Was I to be coddled now? I was formerly the strong and athletic Jack Depaul. Now, I was a corn husk of a man.

I followed Nurse O'Reilly down the aisle. When I reached the steps down to the platform, I hesitated. With crutches under both arms, I stared down at the three steps and took in a deep breath. *Please God, don't let me look like an invalid in front of my wife.* Stairs this steep and narrow were still a challenge for me. At the other stops, the porter had assisted me. There wasn't one now. Nurse O'Reilly, already on the ground, turned back. She would try to help me. She was that type of woman. Did I want that? Before I could decide, Delphia appeared. She stood on the ground looking up at me. I could barely meet her gaze. Sweat trickled down my back despite the bitter cold air that froze the hairs in my nose.

"Jack, welcome home." She smiled and bounded up the stairs to kiss me on the cheek. Even in the outside air, I caught her scent—rose water and lemons. "Do you need help getting down?" She looked into my eyes. I wanted to turn away, to hide.

"No, I'm fine." It was more of a grunt than actual words, but it did the job. She backed away, flushing red. I hated myself for it, but God help me, I was so angry and humiliated. This was what I'd dreaded. Her expression of pity followed by a need to help as if I were a child. I should be strong. I should be the one offering her help. An image of our wedding night played before me. I'd lifted her up as if she weighed nothing to carry her into the room at the inn. What a fool I'd been, thinking I would go overseas and be a hero. Instead, they'd robbed me of my life.

I put the crutches onto a step and then followed with my foot, repeating that three times. The nurses in England where I'd rehabilitated said it would take some time to become an expert, but that soon it would be second nature. None of them had actually ever had a leg amputated, so I'm not sure I trusted what they said. Time would tell. But I'd be damned if I let Delphia be my leg. I would not burden her for the rest of our marriage. However long it lasted, which if it were up to me, would be weeks, not months.

God, she was pretty. I could see how hard she was working to be brave and loving. I was being awful. But I couldn't bring myself to be polite and gracious. I wanted to strike out at the world, scream and hurl my crutches.

At the same time, I wanted to bury my face in her neck and weep like a child and say I was sorry and how much I loved her and that I'd wanted to give her the whole world.

I couldn't say any of those things. She would not be able to leave a man who was pitiful. But a mean one? That was a different story.

"Could you move out of the way? Stop hovering. I won't have a woman fluttering over me night and day."

Her eyes widened, hurt by my tone and my words. She backed away, pale and shaken. No more fake cheer. Good. It was best she faced the truth. We could no longer be a young couple in love. One of us was irreparably changed.

My mother rushed toward us, followed by Papa. I had both crutches placed under my arms and braced myself for the onslaught, stiffening as they stopped in front of me.

"Welcome home, son," Papa said, clasping my shoulders and looking straight into my eyes. "We're glad you're back."

"Sure thing," I said.

Mama, looking apprehensive, asked if it was all right to give me a hug. Why wouldn't it be? I was not a fragile porcelain doll. Her question angered me, though, and I lashed out.

"You might knock me over," I said between clenched teeth.

Mama flinched. "Oh, all right. Later then."

Later? What did that mean?

"We've got the car parked just outside," Papa said. "Not much of a walk at all."

"I can still walk." I lifted a crutch. "That's what this is for. Takes the place of my leg, now doesn't it?" Even I cringed at the bitterness in my voice. But I was hard and cruel now. I could not be any other way.

Delphia beamed at me, perhaps to disguise her shock at my appearance and behavior. "We've got a surprise for you. We finished the house, inside and out. It's all ready for us to move in." Did she not see what was in front of us? Why would she tell me about a house I had no intention of living in? "Wait until you see the details. Our perfect little nest…" She trailed off, most likely in reaction to my stony glare.

"Delphia's already taken all her things out to the house,"

Mama said. "Papa and I brought your things over too. All you have to do is move in and rest."

Not if I had anything to do with it. I was moving back to live at the farm. This marriage had been a mistake. I was not about to ruin Delphia's life. The sooner she understood that, the better.

WE DROVE out of the station with Delphia and my mother chattering away about all of the things they'd done to the cottage. I only half listened, taking in the scenery instead, with my stupid crutches sitting next to me, keeping me apart from my young, vibrant wife.

A lacy layer of snow covered the ground. Everything seemed dull and gray under a close cloud covering. The leafless trees with spindly branches appeared delicate and brittle. Even the beautiful hue of the evergreens did little to make a difference. Good. Everything was as ugly as I felt.

They'd painted the outside of our cottage a butter yellow, with white trim and a black door. I should have been delighted, but it all seemed silly to me. A dollhouse for a broken toy.

Delphia was staring at me with an excited expression on her face. Her cheeks were flushed from the cold and her eyes so blue they almost startled me. She'd grown even lovelier since I'd been gone. If only the same could be said for me. "I hope you like what we chose for the interiors. They're not at all fussy, right, Merry?"

"We chose blues and grays, knowing you like those colors," Mama said.

"Who paid for all of this?" I gestured toward the house as my father parked in the driveway. Shrubs and bushes had been planted in beds, dormant now. A cobblestoned walkway led up to the small front porch.

"It was a wedding gift from my parents," Delphia said. "They wanted it to be nice for you when you came home."

"She's been working night and day, quite literally," Papa said. "You have a strong, diligent young lady here."

Delphia got out of her side of my father's car the moment he turned off the engine. I took the crutches and pushed open my own door, setting my only foot on the icy ground and heaving myself up and out of the car.

My wife stood by, watching and wringing her hands. "Do you need anything?"

"I'm fine. You don't need to help me in or out of the car." When I'd gotten in earlier, she'd hovered close by, ready to assist me if I needed her. I didn't. I wouldn't. I was no charity case. No child to be petted and placed in and out of a car.

My crutches made small prints in the icy layer of snow in between my solo footstep. I looked away toward the house. That's when I first saw it. A ramp. They'd put a ramp in for the cripple?

Delphia, always observant, noticed where my gaze went. "We were able to add it just a few days ago. To make it a little easier for you." Her voice shook. I'd made my own wife nervous.

I didn't say anything, simply walked up the ramp onto the porch. Delphia had run ahead on her lithe legs and now stood holding the door for me, which opened to a hallway with the living room on one side and a den on the other. I moved past her into our living room. It was gorgeous, modern and bright with a blue couch and a gray-and-white-patterned rug over shining wood floors. They'd spruced up the fireplace, adding a new walnut mantel and replacing a few of the bricks that had been cracked or broken. A rocking chair, painted white, was in the corner, waiting for Delphia and a baby.

I glanced to the right. The den now had a large desk, also made of walnut, positioned near a window. A lamp gave off a soft yellow light.

"Phillip made this desk for you." Delphia ran her hand over the surface of the desk. It was obviously from Phillip. The great attention to detail on the dovetail joints that attached the legs to the tabletop could only have been done by him.

"Must be a fine thing to spend your time sanding wood," I said, snarling like a rabid dog. "I was too busy traipsing through swamps to think of such things."

Delphia's hand flew to her mouth. She stared at me with horrified eyes. She'd never known me to be cruel. She better get used to it. This was the new me.

"He fought in the first one, you know," Delphia said. "Almost died and then came home only to get really sick. I hardly think he's the one to be angry with."

"Who then?" My eyebrows twitched, and the muscles in my cheeks tightened. Controlling the rage that coursed through me was impossible.

Mama and Papa were also watching me, obviously distraught and shocked by my behavior. Or was it the way I looked? Gaunt and weak with dead eyes? I knew. I'd seen myself in the mirror that very morning. The hollowness of my cheeks and dullness of my skin. Delphia wouldn't know me, I'd thought. She wouldn't want to know me.

"Hitler, perhaps?" Delphia's eyes snapped. I could practically hear them crackle. "The Japanese? But not Phillip. Not anyone here, who have all been praying and praying for your safe return."

"I've returned." My crutches creaked as I hurried down the hallway. The kitchen came into view. Painted bright yellow with pine cabinets and lacy white curtains at the windows and a cheery breakfast nook in the corner. Across the hallway in the dining room, a long table covered with a white cloth filled up most of the space. A bouquet of twigs, pine branches, and red berries sat in the middle. It was set for dinner. Two plates with white china dishes. Where had those come from?

"You have been busy," I said.

"Do you like it?" Delphia asked.

"What's the upstairs like?" I asked, glancing at the stairway up to the second floor. Would I even be able to get up there? Not now, anyway. I was suddenly exhausted.

"You must be tired," Delphia said. "Come sit in the living room. I'll get us all some tea. Lizzie sent over those molasses cookies you used to love when we were kids."

My mouth watered. The food had been so bad over there. Not only the confiscated rice and dried fish, but later when supplies came, the K rations had been disgusting. Glutinous and fatty tin cans of meat, hard-as-a-rock biscuits, slimy green beans. If we hadn't been so hungry, I'm sure we would have rejected it on texture alone.

"For dinner, I've made a roast," Delphia said. "Lizzie taught me how to cook while you were gone. Aren't you surprised and pleased with me?"

"Not really. You can do anything you set your mind to. Always has been that way."

Delphia glowed from my compliment. I was a nasty, mean man to make my innocent wife so delighted over a few kind words. A slap of guilt reverberated through me. But no, I must be this way. I must be impossible to be around so that she could walk away without feeling responsible. No one could blame her if she left a man without a limb who was mean as a snake. It wouldn't be hard at all. No effort required whatsoever to be as mean as I felt.

They were all looking at one another as if I weren't in the room. "I'd like to take a nap," I said flatly.

"Oh, well, of course." Delphia moved toward the stairwell. "I can show you up to our room. Or...can you get up there with the crutches?" The sheer panic in her eyes hurt worse than anything had yet today.

"I can get up the stairs. And down for that matter. If I feel like coming down for dinner, I will."

"I can bring you a tray," Delphia said. "It's no problem. I know you're tired and in need of a good meal. We'll have you feeling strong again in no time."

I stared at her, letting my eyes bore into her. "If you truly think I'll ever be strong again, then you're more delusional than I thought." I placed my crutches on the bottom step and started the long journey upstairs.

When I reached the second floor, I looked right and left. The larger of the two bedrooms had obviously been made for the happily married couple Delphia thought we were, with a double bed covered with a flower-patterned quilt. Thick curtains in a pine green were pulled back from windows that looked out to the backyard. Chunky side tables were paired with a manly leather chair and ottoman. She'd made this room for us. For me, actually, with my favorite colors and tastes in mind.

I looked to the smaller room. There were twin beds covered with red quilts and a dresser painted a royal blue. A small table and miniature chairs had been placed in front of the window. I recognized it from Quinn and Alexander's home. It had been Addie and Delphia's table when they were small. When I'd visited them as a kid, we'd drawn pictures and looked at books. It had been refinished and painted the same blue. A rocking chair near the window, made from cherrywood, appeared new. Another of Phillip's creations, perhaps? All of this made for the children Delphia thought we would have. My fists clenched. A bitter, acrid taste filled my mouth. *I will not have it*, I thought. *She must be set right.* There would be no children. No marriage. She would be free to live here with whomever she chose. All I knew is that it would not be me.

Then I went into the room with the twin beds and closed the door.

14

DELPHIA

The thumping sound of my husband's crutches on the stairs echoed through the house. I stared at the empty space he'd just occupied, unsure of what I'd just witnessed. Or who had just been in my kitchen. What had just happened? Who was this stranger in my house? Not Jack.

Blindly, barely aware that my in-laws followed, I left the hallway and went into the living room. A fire in the hearth warmed the room. Regardless, I shivered violently.

Merry sat on the edge of the couch, clasping and unclasping her hands.

Harley dropped into the leather easy chair. I'd ordered two, imagining Jack and myself right here by the fire on a cold winter's evening, growing old together.

"Not sure what to say here," Harley said. "That was not my son."

"Yes, he's not himself," Merry said in a tone that told me she was trying to convince herself, not me. "You mustn't take what he said to heart."

"He looked at me with hatred in his eyes," I said, trying not to cry. My chest and stomach ached as if someone had stabbed me over and over with a dull knife. "It's as if he no longer loves me." What would I do now? Live here with a man who despises me simply because I represent the life he wanted, the one he thought he would come back to? I was healthy and athletic, bounding here and there. Until today, I'd thought that's what he would want and need. Instead, he rejected me at every turn.

"It's not true," Merry said. "He's hurting. He thinks you won't want him, so he's pushing you away before you can run away."

"I'd never run from him," I said. "We're married." I set my jaw, my natural stubbornness replacing some of the pain. "I'll be here for him until he comes back around. I'll not let him push me out of our home."

"He's nearly unrecognizable," Harley said. "That hair and beard. He indeed looks like he's lived in a jungle for a year."

That was the truth. I'd been shocked to my very core at the sight of him coming off the train. His hair was long and disheveled. He had a beard that covered most of his face. Even his eyes were different. Still blue but no longer shiny. The eyes of a dead man. *What have they done to you, my darling?*

"He'll come around," Merry said. "Once he rests. And shaves that awful beard, cuts his hair, and puts on one of his old suits for church. He'll see that everything here's the same and that we're all so happy to have him home."

Harley rubbed his eyes with the heels of his hands. "I don't know. It doesn't matter that we haven't changed, he has." He looked over at me. "This might be the fight of your life. He's going to be awful to live with for a while. You have to stay by him, even if he's ugly to you."

"What if he doesn't want me to?" I asked, unable to shake the cold glint of Jack's eyes.

"It's his pride, my dear," Harley said. "He feels he's let you down and that you'll be better off without him." He rose to his feet and came to stand next to me by the fire. "You married him for better or worse. This will test your character and your marriage. But remember, you two—you've been best friends for a long time. He needs you now more than ever."

"I'll do my very best," I said, meaning every word. My eyes filled with tears. "I was looking forward to seeing him more than I've ever wanted anything in my life. I couldn't care less about his leg. He came home alive. That's all I've prayed for these many months."

"As have I," Merry said. "Did we ask God for the wrong thing?"

"No, you didn't," Harley said. "You two must keep the faith. He needs his wife and his mother right now more than he ever has. With you two by his side, he *will* heal mentally and physically. We have to believe in him more than he believes in himself right now."

I nodded and moved over to the couch to sit by my mother-in-law. I took her cold hand in mine and squeezed. "We can do this. My mother will help, too. We'll find the real Jack again."

"God help us, I hope so," Merry said.

MY MOTHER and father arrived shortly after Merry and Harley, who still had chores to do and dinner to make, had left for home. Even though I wished they would stay for dinner, I knew it was too much to ask of them. They'd given up several hours of work already today. However, my parents must have known I needed them, because no sooner had I stoked the fire and taken the roast out of the oven than I heard their car in the driveway.

I didn't wait for them to come to the door, running outside to greet them. My mother carried a cake tin. I threw myself against her anyway, wrapping my arms around her and bursting into tears, crying into her shoulder, the tin pressing into my chest. "He's awful, Mama. Mean and growly like a bear."

"What?" She glanced over at my father, who stood looking at

the house, as if there were answers to our problems inside the cozy spaces. I knew there were not.

"Tell us everything," Mama said quietly. "Before we go in."

I dried my tears and explained what had happened, the knot in my stomach growing tighter with every word. When I was done, my father drew me into an embrace, kissing the top of my head. "You will be fine, love. He needs time and consistent love from you. Men are not good at being unwell, I'm afraid. This is a terrible blow to him. You must be patient."

"I'll do my best," I said, echoing what I'd said earlier to my in-laws. "I thought he'd be so pleased about the house. It was foolish to think so. I can see that now. All he can see or feel is his injury." The truth about the state of my husband's health filled me with a dark, ominous dread. How would we possibly get through this together if he wanted to shut me out of his life?

MAMA HELPED me fix a tray of the roast beef, potatoes, and carrots. I'd made American-style biscuits to go with them. How proud I'd been when they'd come out fluffy and flaky, just as Lizzie had taught me. It seemed stupid now.

After giving me another hug, my parents left, giving me further hugs and kisses and promises they would check on us tomorrow. That left me alone to take Jack's supper to him. The table I'd carefully laid for dinner would not be used. Not tonight, but maybe tomorrow. I must press onward.

Still, I fought tears as I climbed the stairs. The reunion I'd imagined was not to be. My parents hadn't even been able to see him. After all the months away and all their worries and prayers, he hadn't given them the courtesy of a greeting. When I reached the second floor, I realized he'd left the door to our bedroom open. A good sign?

My hopes were quickly dashed. Our bed was untouched,

which meant he'd gone into the spare. The one I'd hoped would be our children's room. He'd gone in there instead of our marriage bedroom.

My legs wobbled and my breath hitched. If he were trying to send a message, it certainly worked. An ache at the back of my throat made it hard to swallow. Tears pressed against the backs of my eyes. *Do not cry*, I told myself. *It is all right. You're all right. Give him his dinner.*

I knocked on the door to the smaller room and waited, listening for sounds of life. None came. "Jack, I have your dinner."

"Leave it by the door." More of the growling he'd done earlier.

"No, I'm coming in." Swallowing hard, I turned the knob and opened the door a crack. He was sitting in the rocking chair by the window, staring out into the darkness. From this angle and in the dim light, he looked as if he were unharmed. Other than his shaggy hair and that ugly beard, I would not have known the changes that had stolen his spirit.

"I told you to leave it." He didn't even turn to look at me.

"And I told you I was coming in." I put the tray on the child's table Phillip had refinished and painted—the same one where all of my siblings had spent many happy afternoons. I'd been touched when Mama suggested I take it for my new home. Like a fool, I'd imagined the children Jack and I would have sitting in the small chairs, laughing and bickering and teasing one another just as we had.

I stood there on weak legs, watching him, with my arms crossed tightly over my chest. I'd worn a light blue dress with a flattering neckline that I thought he would like, but he'd barely looked at me. "How long will this continue?" I asked, sharply, forgetting already my vow to be loving and patient.

"Not long." He slowly turned to look at me with those flat, dead eyes.

"Good. I'll expect you to get on with things, as people do—as people are doing as we speak. I don't need to remind you of the boys on the front line still, fighting for freedom and possibly dying as we sit here smelling my roast beef."

"I'm not hungry."

"That's impossible. You're skinny as a rail." How many times had he written to tell me how much he missed his mother's cooking, all of which had spurred on my determination to improve my skills? On our wedding night, he'd teased me that he didn't care if I could cook, as long as I kept loving him.

Where had that man gone?

He turned away, peering out the window once more, and said, "We need to talk."

"I expect so." My stomach twisted with nerves. What would he say? That he didn't want me anymore? That he would be sleeping apart from me?

"I want a divorce."

The knot in my stomach unfurled and spilled throughout my body, cold and bitter and black. I staggered slightly. I'd not thought he would ever say such a thing to me. Or anyone, for that matter. People who married for love didn't ask for divorces less than a year later.

"But why?" I whispered, my bravado from earlier vanishing. "Why would you cast me aside when you need me most?"

He whirled his head around. "I don't need you. I'm perfectly capable of living my life without the help of a skinny woman."

That cut. He knew I was self-conscious about my scrawny figure. He wanted to hurt me, I realized. That might have been the worst realization yet. My sweet, kind, sensitive Jack had turned as mean as a beaten, starving dog. That's what they'd done to him, I thought. They'd treated him as poorly as a dog no one wanted or cared for, and he'd become one.

Unshed tears made my lower lip quiver and my head ache. I clenched my teeth and drew in a ragged breath. "This is not what we vowed to do. We vowed for better or worse. What if it was me? Would you leave me because I was no longer..." No longer what? Perfect? Whole? Able-bodied?

"Attractive? Virile? Is that what you want to say?" He stared at me through narrowed eyes.

"You're still attractive to me, you fool," I sputtered. "It has nothing to do with your injury."

"My injury? Is that what we're calling it? Say the truth. They blew apart my leg and now I have a hideous stump." He pulled on the fabric of his trousers, which he had tied into a knot. "Call it what it is. I'm now a cripple. Useless for anything. I can't ride a horse, or chop wood or hoe a garden or take you out dancing." His eyes reddened and tears leaked from his eyes. My heart softened, seeing him like this. I'd rather it had been me. He would have been all right taking care of me, but not the other way around.

"Why can't you just let me love you?" I asked. "That's all I want. We can make it through this and find joy again. We can have a family. You'll learn how to do whatever you choose once you have more time."

"Delphia, no," he said, his tone as hard as stone.

"You should be more concerned with that atrocious beard and hair," I said, ignoring him. "Which makes you look like a bum, not the man I married. In fact, it has nothing to do with your missing leg. Is that better?" Sarcasm dripped from my voice now. Already he had turned me into a bitter shrew. "Is it all right to call it a missing leg rather than an injury?"

"This is how I choose to look now. They made me into an animal, and I shall stay that way."

"Divorce?" There, I'd said it out loud. *Divorce*. Such a despicable word. One I never thought would be associated with Jack and me. How was it possible that a little over a year ago we'd been entwined in each other's arms? "Do you even know how to get a divorce?" I asked.

He blinked and jerked his head back, as if he'd not thought of this practicality before. "I can find out."

"I'll make it impossible for you. You have to prove there's a reason for it, like adultery or neglect. I've done neither. What I've done is make a beautiful home for us." I started to cry then, which made me even angrier. "You've broken my heart, Jack Depaul. I deserve much more than this. I would never have deserted you, no matter how you came home to me."

With the aid of his crutches, he jerked upright and pounded one crutch into the wood floor. He roared at me, as if I'd awakened a demon. "That's what I'm telling you. This is for you. To be rid of me. I can't bear to be a burden to you. Can't you understand that?" He was surprisingly good with the crutches, standing straight and tall with them under his arms.

"You're not a burden, but you *are* mean as a snake. If you want to push me away, then you're off to a good start." Would there be any love left in me by the time he was done?

"I'm moving back in with my parents. Tomorrow."

I tried like mad to control my tears and not sob, but they rose up out of me, shaking my entire body. How could he be so cruel? I'd done nothing but love him as if my life depended on it. Maybe it did. I could no longer speak and could barely breathe through my sobs.

His head drooped and he spoke softly, his voice hoarse from shouting. "We can both agree you deserve better than the man I've become."

"Yes, but it has nothing to do with your missing leg and everything to do with your cruelty. If you want a divorce, then go ahead. Leave me. Leave this marriage and the vows we said before God and everyone we love. If that's the man you've become, then yes, I deserve better."

I left the room, slamming the door behind me but leaving the tray of food. As angry and hurt as I was, I really wanted him to eat something. If he no longer wanted me to be his wife, then

I would have to learn to live again without him. I truly couldn't fathom how it was possible. Regardless, no matter how angry I was, I would never wish him harm. More than anything, I wanted him to be happy.

Once downstairs, I went to the kitchen and wept with my head hanging over the sink, letting the tears fall in with the dirty pans. When my eyes were no longer capable of tears, I looked around my new, bright kitchen, feeling as helpless as a lost child. The roast was still in its pan, cooling so that the fat had begun to congeal around the potatoes and carrots. What was I supposed to do now? I couldn't stay here, not with him. I'd go home to my parents and sleep in my own bed. Addie would come to be with me in the big bed we used to share when one of us needed the other. Tonight, she could comfort me while I cried my eyes out. I'd done the same for her once upon a time. Although she and James had had their happy ending. I'd already had the bliss and joy that love could bring. Now I was to face the devastation that came with losing love. I wished to God I'd never fallen in love with him in the first place.

15

JACK

I heard the front door shut and looked out the window to see Delphia with her coat on heading to the car. She was leaving. Good. That's what I wanted. She should go back to her parents. Once I was home with mine, she could return and live here in this house she'd carefully put together. Even in the state I was in, I could not help but notice all the fine details. Phillip's presence was here, as were the rest of her family. They'd all come together for me.

For the first time, I noticed the children's books on the shelf opposite the bed. They must have been hers and Addie's when they were young. She'd brought them over here with such hope.

I hated myself. I hated God.

She'd put the tray of food on the child's table, making it impossible for me to reach. This was a perfect example of why we could no longer be together. She had no idea what it was like to be in my position. All of the ways I needed to adapt would mean she would have to as well. She was young and so beautiful and witty and charming—she would find another man by this time next year.

Where would that leave me?

Moving back home was only a temporary solution to what I should do with the rest of my life. I could no longer help Papa at the farm, thus making it impossible for me to live there. I was a man who earned his keep, not a leech who sucked the life from others.

I'd move away from here. Go to Denver, maybe, and get a job and live alone for the rest of my life. It would be better for everyone. What kind of job could I do, though? I had no education other than horse breeding. I was no good to anyone without my physical prowess.

How did one get a divorce? I hadn't really thought all of that through when I told Delphia my intention. She had not abandoned me or committed adultery. What was I to do about it? If she wouldn't agree to a divorce then I wouldn't have much power to do what I wanted. Which was to be done with this marriage. Right? Yes, it was. For her. She deserved to be happy with a man who could give her everything. I had nothing. How would I support her and a family? She'd have to work to keep us afloat while I withered away in this house. No, I couldn't do it. *Wouldn't* do it to her.

For God's sake, I couldn't even drive a car. I was as helpless as a baby.

Despite my protestations to the contrary, I was very hungry. The dinner she'd lovingly prepared for me was probably cold by now. Still, it would be better than anything I'd had since I left here. I hobbled over to the table. Putting as much weight as I could on my good side, with the crutches tucked under my arms, I leaned over, but it was too far. Why had she put it here?

Forget it. I didn't need food. I would use the toilet and then go to bed. Tomorrow, my mother would help with all of this. I would explain to her what I needed. And then I would start my life over without Delphia.

I WAS in bed when I heard the car in the driveway, lying on my right side with my head on the pillow. Even without my missing leg, I was much too big for the bed. My good foot hung off the end.

I heard the squeak of the front door opening, followed by Delphia's quick steps down the hallway and up the stairs. Why was she back? Hadn't she gotten the message? I didn't want her here.

A knock pounded on the bedroom door. "It's me. I'm coming in."

I sighed but said nothing. Couldn't she leave well enough alone?

"I realized, driving home to my parents', that it would be hard for you to reach the plate." Her skin was flushed pink. She was pretty. So very pretty. Even when she was mad as a hornet at me.

But she'd figured it out about the plate of food. Leave it to her. What hadn't been obvious at first had then occurred to her. A flicker of hope ignited in me, but I quickly crushed it. No, this was not fair to her. She was already accommodating me by turning around and trying to make things right. This was her. Kind and smart, always thinking of what I needed and wanted. I could not ruin her life, too.

She marched over to the little table and picked up the tray. "I'm an idiot. I don't know what I was thinking. Let me heat this for you, and I'll bring it back up. You can eat in bed there with the tray on your lap."

I should have protested, but I was weak from hunger. Instead, I nodded. "No need to heat it up."

She looked down at the tray and made a face. "No, it's not good this way. It looks disgusting with the fat congealing like that."

"If you'd seen the K rations, you would know it looks like a feast."

Her brow furrowed as she looked at me and then back at the tray. "Give me a moment. I'll be back."

For the next fifteen minutes, the sound of her movements in the kitchen below kept me company. How I'd longed to hear this very thing for all the months I was away. How could I possibly let her go when everything in me longed for her? Because that's what a man does when he loves a woman. He puts her needs first. That is what I would do.

———————

WHEN SHE RETURNED with a steaming plate of food, my mouth watered. I sat up, despite my intention to remain impassive. She'd put the dinner on a new kind of tray, one that folded at the ends to make a sort of table.

"Where did you get this?" I asked. "The table, I mean."

"I borrowed it from Jo. Phillip made it when their oldest broke her leg. I forgot I had it earlier. I was flustered." She swept a stray lock of hair from her forehead. "I'm sorry I was so thoughtless. I didn't think. It was terrible."

"Not your fault. I should have said something. Anyway, I'm not hungry."

"For heaven's sake, don't be ridiculous. You told me in your letters that you yearned for food from home." She gestured toward the pot roast, which smelled of rosemary and red wine. "Eat. I'll come back and get that when you're done since you obviously don't want me here."

"Thank you, I will," I said stiffly. Misery and regret for my behavior made my stomach churn. Could I eat this without being sick?

"Go on now." She didn't say anything further, leaving the room and shutting the door behind her.

I dug into the dinner, suddenly unable to resist the scent of slow-cooked beef. The first bite made me groan out loud with pleasure. Real food. Home-cooked. By Delphia of all people. She'd learned to cook for me, even when she'd said she could not be that kind of wife. Here she was now, too, making sure I had a warm meal, even though I'd been awful to her.

It might have been the best meal I'd ever tasted. Lizzie had really taught her well. My independent woman who claimed she had no use for cooking and cleaning and other household duties. What had made her change her mind?

Love, you imbecile, a voice whispered to me.

AN HOUR LATER, knuckles rapping on the door woke me from a doze. It was Delphia, come to fetch my tray. The lamp remained on, but the room had a hazy, dreamlike feel.

"I'm sorry to wake you," she said softly. "But I should take the dirty dishes." Leaning over me, she took the tray from the bed and set it on the dresser. "I'm going to get you extra blankets. It's going to be cold tonight."

A few moments later, she returned with two wool blankets. I was lying on my back. staring up at the ceiling. She spread the first one out over me and then the other. "Is there anything else you need before I go to bed?"

I peered up at her face. Her cheeks had hollowed since I'd left. She'd grown even thinner during my time away. Dark smudges under her eyes hinted at fatigue. In the last letter I'd gotten from my mother she had mentioned how hard Delphia was working. I'd not been the only one to suffer. I knew that. Of course, I did. But I still couldn't be so selfish as to ask a woman like Delphia to look after me the rest of her life. I was an invalid now. Useless to her or anyone.

"I'm fine, thank you." I could be polite at least. "The dinner was really good. It might be the best I've ever had."

"You must have been hungry then." A slight smile lifted her mouth and for a moment, she looked like the old, ambitious, full-of-life woman I'd married. How I loved her smile. It had been imprinted upon my soul, that smile. Just as every other element that made up the woman I'd been so desperately in love with.

"Lizzie taught you well." My curiosity got the better of me. I had to ask. "What made you decide to learn to cook?"

She lifted her delicate chin and crossed her arms over her chest. A protective move, I thought. "I wanted to surprise you, I guess. Make a home for you to return to, one in which you were warm and well-fed and properly looked after. A home like my mother has always run."

"Only she had a Lizzie."

Another half-smile lit up her eyes. "Perhaps more like your mother, then."

It was true. An image of Mama in the mornings when I was in high school came to mind. An early riser, she and Papa had already been working for hours by the time I made my way downstairs, dressed for school. She'd always had a hot breakfast for us. "Can't send you out to the world with an empty stomach," she'd said. I'd often wondered how she could time the cooking of eggs to match my appearance at the kitchen table. My mother had always made everything nice for us, even in the lean years when Papa was still building the business.

"Regardless, it was delicious." I shifted slightly, uncomfortable, wishing I could sleep on my left side as I'd done all my life. But without my leg, it felt too strange to do so.

"What can I do for you?" Delphia, obviously sensing my agitation, moved closer. "Are you in pain?"

"Not too bad. Sometimes my ghost leg aches. Or itches. It's the damnedest thing."

She winced at the curse word. I don't know that she'd ever heard me say a bad word before. I'd learned that in the marines too.

"I'm sorry," I said.

She reached down to the end of the bed to smooth out the spare blanket over my good foot. "It's all right. I suppose you've been with some rough men all these months. You're bound to pick up a few bad habits."

"You've no idea."

She looked at me with a queer expression on her face, one of sorrow and anger all mixed together. "That's right, I don't. I've thought all this time that given the chance—if you made it out alive—you would tell it all to me. Like you once did. When we were still happy. Before this blasted war." The last part she said more to herself than to me.

I avoided her gaze, fixing upon the painting that hung on the wall. It was of three little girls at the ocean, playing in the surf. I'd not seen it before. "Where did that come from?" I asked.

Her gaze traveled to the painting. "I bought it from a gallery in Denver. It reminded me of my sisters. I thought it would bring good luck into a room I intended would be for our children." She looked down at her hands, speaking quietly. "Anyway, I'll let you sleep. I have an early day tomorrow and should get some rest myself."

Don't go, I wanted to say. *Stay with me. Lie with me. Stroke my hair. Tell me everything's going to be all right.* "I'll move to my parents' tomorrow."

A spasm of pain pinched her features. "Fine. But one thing I wanted to ask—what about a prosthetic? Wouldn't it help with mobility?"

"I don't want one. I told them no." I avoided her gaze, turning back to the painting.

"But why?"

I pulled the quilt closer to my neck. "Because they're disgusting and they never fit right and hurt."

"All right, if that's what you want." She sighed, bringing her hand to her mouth, acting as if she wanted to say something further, but she didn't. "Good night, Jack." She turned to go, and again I wanted to call her back to me. Instead, I closed my eyes and waited for the sound of her footsteps to leave the room and cross the hall.

Exhausted mentally and physically, I thought I would fall asleep easily. How many times had I wished for a bed with clean sheets and a soft mattress when I'd been away? Every single night. I'd slept on the ground covered with leaves more times than I could count. In the days of battle, we'd not been able to get more than an hour or so of sleep for fear a sniper would take us out. One must be ever diligent to stay alive. I'd been so, and still they'd gotten me.

It was so quiet here. No sounds of other men or the horrible shrill of bullets or crashing of bombs. Regardless, I'd resigned myself. The sounds of war would stay with me. All my life, I'd be haunted by them.

It was so quiet here. Snow fell outside the windows in silence, padding the ground with one soft flake after another. There was no wind tonight, either. I listened, hoping to hear an owl hooting in the woods around the cottage. Instead, I heard a soft whinny of a noise coming from the room across the hall. Delphia, trying to cry silently. I'd broken her heart. I was a bastard. My stomach clenched with guilt. But this was the way it had to be. I had to remain cold, or she would sacrifice her life for me. I would not have it. I would not succumb to my guilt or my love for the woman I'd planned to spend the rest of my life with. To do so would only open us to further hurt.

I turned over onto my stomach and hugged the pillow, determined to endure the muffled sounds of my wife crying.

Finally, she stopped. She'd cried herself to sleep, all alone in the big bed.

Sleep did not come for me until the wee hours of the morning. When it finally did, I dreamt of shells and bombs and the shouting of men in pain. They called out for their mothers. That's how I knew they were dying.

I was already dead. No more crying out for me.

16

DELPHIA

The sound of someone screaming woke me from a dreamless, bone-weary sleep. I shot straight up from the warmth of the feather comforter. Jack. It was Jack. I threw back the covers. Cold air smacked me as it always did on winter mornings. I glanced at the clock. It was nearly five. Without bothering to put on my robe, I hustled in my stocking feet across the hall. I'd left my door open in case he needed anything but had cried myself to sleep. Now, I wish I'd stayed awake to be there when he needed me.

The light from the hallway was enough to see the shadow of his body, but I turned on a lamp anyway. I needed to see him if I were to help him.

He was scrambling about, crying out, "Stop. Just stop. Please God have mercy."

I went to his side and placed a hand on his shoulder. "Jack, wake up."

His hands came up out of the covers, punching the air. His eyes popped open. For a second, it was obvious he didn't know where he was or who had wakened him. But slowly, the realization that it was me came to his eyes. "Delphia?"

"You were dreaming," I said softly. My fingers brushed strands of long hair from his damp forehead.

"Nightmares. I'm sorry if I woke you." He sounded young then and untarnished. Sleep still had him in its clutches. His armor had not yet been pulled over to hide his true self. A stab of love and longing for him almost brought me to my knees. Despite all the changes in him, he still smelled like Jack. My Jack. My love.

"Don't be. What can I do for you?" I whispered. "Anything at all? I'll do whatever I can to help."

His eyes were bright, almost feverish when he stared up at me. "Is it morning?"

I perched on the side of the narrow bed, inches from him. My fingers itched to touch him further, but I regained control of myself. "Jack, you don't have to leave. I want you to stay. Give it a little time…give us a little time to adjust." It took everything in me to say those words. He'd already humiliated and rejected me enough for a lifetime yesterday, but I had to try. Last night, I'd asked God to guide me, to give me insight to save my marriage. When I woke just now, the answer had not come because all I could think of was getting to him and pulling him out of the nightmare. Now, however, the answer seemed clear. I had to put my pride aside and make sure he knew I wanted him to stay. "I want you to give us a chance, Jack. I want a chance."

"A chance for what?" His eyes glittered in the lamplight.

"A chance for me to prove how much I love you—to show you there's nothing in this world that would keep me from wanting you."

He flung an arm over his face as if the sight of me hurt him. "I can't ever let you see what I look like now. My leg—my stump —will revolt you."

I started to cry tears of frustration. *How do I get through to him?* I asked God. *Guide me, please.*

146

He removed his arm and looked into my eyes. "I'm sorry I'm hurting you. It's the last thing I want."

"Then why are you doing it?"

"I would rather do that than have you feel pity for me. If I thought you would stay because you felt sorry for me—that's the worst thing I can imagine."

"Instead, you're trying to hurt me enough that I start to hate you? I beg your pardon, but that's really stupid."

"I'm trying to protect you."

"From what?" I asked.

"From having your life ruined, just as mine is."

"It's not, though. You're here. You can have as full a life as you want. The only thing that could have ruined my life is if you'd died over there. Or if you go through with a divorce. You're my life, Jack. I swore to love you forever, and I will. I don't care if you have an ugly stump or even that awful beard." I placed my hand on his chest. "You're still in there. I know you are. I'm not giving up on you."

"You will. Eventually."

"Try me, Jack. Show me all of you."

"Get out. Now!" He shouted the last part and made me jump. My heart raced as I slid from the bed to stand on shaking legs.

"I'll go. For now. But I'll see you later. I expect you downstairs for breakfast." Holding my breath, I walked out of the room and across the hallway to my bedroom. I sat on the edge of my own bed and drew in breath after breath to steady myself. Once I'd gathered my emotions and tucked them away, I went downstairs to make the morning meal. If he didn't come down, I'd charge right back up the stairs with a tray. If he could play this game, so could I.

147

I'D JUST PUT the last piece of bacon on a plate when I heard the thumping of Jack's crutches on the stairs. Having set two places at the small kitchen table without much hope that he would join me, I'd fixed breakfast anyhow, frying up flapjacks and bacon and scrambled eggs. Bacon was a true treat. It would have taken me seven ration stamps to get a pound of bacon, and I didn't have enough after splurging on the roast beef. However, Lizzie had bacon in the freezer back at the big house that had come from the slaughter of one of our own pigs from last summer. Since I had no sugar, I'd decided on flapjacks made with whole wheat flour. Lizzie had also sent over a jar of blackberry jam, a little tarter than our usual batches because of the lack of sugar. With so few supplies, we were all making do without cookies or cakes. A small sacrifice for the war effort, of course.

The government had encouraged us to grow Victory Gardens to compensate for the lack of produce. Many in our community had always grown a garden, including all my siblings and of course our gardener at the big house. However, Cymbeline had taken up the Victory Garden challenge with her usual fervor. Worried about the frail and poor, she'd convinced us all to plant much larger gardens than we normally would. She'd pored over a farming guide about best times to plant and what kind of soil worked for certain vegetables to come up with a master plan.

Starting last spring, we'd all carried out her instructions and were quite pleased with the results of our farming efforts. Cym could be a little bossy, but we didn't care. We all had our strengths in our family, and hers had always been mastering the outdoors. Whether it be in athletics or growing bounty from God's earth, she was our girl. All in all, we were doing well. After learning of the tight rationing of meat and vegetables, we'd had a family meeting and decided we would each grow more than our usual amounts and can much of it for winter. As a family, with the garden at the big house and the green thumbs of all my sisters, we had more than enough fresh vegetables and fruit for our family and anyone else in need. Between my sisters and sisters-in-law, we had more than enough potatoes, carrots, onions, squash, and green beans to distribute to anyone who needed them.

We all kept chickens for eggs and grew chicks into fryers as well. I'd only just started my adventure with a chicken coop. While we were working on the house last spring, Viktor and Phillip had put together a small chicken coop for me while Cym and I readied the garden. I had only a half dozen layers, but so far they were doing their job very well, including the eggs I was currently scrambling. It's as if they knew I needed them to help fatten up my husband.

I'd just turned from the stove when he appeared in the doorway. I did a double take. His face was newly shaven. The ugly beard was no more. Standing before me was the clean-cut man I'd married. Other than that long hair and the gauntness of his face, he looked almost like his old self. Hopefully, we could take care of that at the barbershop in town.

A pair of trousers and a freshly pressed shirt hung on his skinny frame. "You found the clothes in the closet then?" I asked.

"Yes. Thank you."

He'd gone into the bedroom to find them. Was this an answer to prayer? And he'd shaved. Progress, perhaps? "You shaved your beard."

"It was itchy."

I waited for him to say more, but instead, he hobbled to the window, peering out at the freshly fallen snow.

"Are you hungry?" I asked. "These are eggs from our very own chickens." I couldn't help but smile with pride. "And I've grown vegetables out back. Josephine and Mama taught me how to can last summer." I gestured toward the pantry, where rows of beans and tomatoes took up an entire shelf. "We've got potatoes in the cellar that will last us all winter if we're careful. Carrots and onions, too."

"I wondered how you got the beef."

"I used my rations. I don't need much if it's just me, so I saved however many I could for when you got home." I couldn't help but feel pleased. "When I got the telegram, I thought it was time to use the ones I'd saved for meat."

"Clever of you." He sounded less angry. I caught a hint of admiration in his voice. How I'd taken it for granted all those years. I'd assumed he'd always think I was wonderful as he had when we were young. He'd always looked at me as if the sun came up every morning because of me. The look of love and appreciation with which he'd looked at me, especially after I came home and we had those short weeks together, had given me more joy and contentment than I'd thought possible. Those days were past. Now, I had a mean and angry man in the house I'd planned so carefully.

A pang of sadness hit me so hard, I had to hold onto the back of the chair. I breathed deep to keep myself from starting up with all the boohooing again.

"Are you all right?" Jack asked, coming all the way into the kitchen. "Are you ill?"

I looked up at him, surprised to see concern in his eyes. A glimpse of the old Jack? Dare I hope? "I'm fine. I was remembering how you used to look at me before you left and wishing I could have just one more day with that man." I knew the moment I said it that I'd made a mistake.

His face flushed purple. A vein in his neck pulsed. "That's exactly what I've been telling you. That man is no longer around. The one here before you is not the man you married. You've got that correct anyway."

Suddenly, I was exhausted. I'd not slept well, and he'd woken me so early. When was the last time I'd eaten? I'd not been able to force any dinner down last night. Not after the horrific day I'd had. I sank into one of the kitchen chairs and helped myself to a piece of bacon and some eggs. "I don't care what you do," I said. "But I can't remember the last meal I had. If you want to stay—then stay. If not, I'll go ahead and take care of myself."

He stared at me with his mouth slightly open before going to the table and sitting at the place I'd set for him. I tried not to notice how precarious he seemed as he lowered into the chair, but it was impossible not to see that he was hurting by the way he gritted his teeth. He was still getting used to making it around with one leg and the crutches, but in time it would be better. If he could get stronger, then things would be easier for him.

Jack plopped eggs and a flapjack onto his plate and took two pieces of bacon. "You look like you hardly eat anything."

"I eat." I flushed. I'd hoped he wouldn't notice how scrawny I'd become. "I've been busy. There are people here in town who need the food more than I do anyway."

"Sounds to me like you've done the work of three men since I've been gone." He bit into the bacon and closed his eyes, groaning slightly. "That's good."

I remembered the coffee I'd brewed and got up to pour us each a cup. We'd have to enjoy it black. Since the war, I saved only a small amount of milk for cooking. "It helped to keep occupied, especially if it was something for you, like this house or the garden." I set the cup in front of him.

He smelled it first before taking a sip. "Also good."

We ate in silence. I started to feel a little better as the nourishment spread throughout my body. I pushed my plate away and started in on my coffee. I'd not grown fond of drinking it black, but I didn't complain about it, not when there were real problems. Someday, when the war was over, we would have cream again.

Would I be drinking it alone?

"I can show you the garden and chicken coop after breakfast," I said.

"Not necessary. I'll be calling my mother after this to tell her to come get me."

The kitchen wasn't particularly warm, but I had a sudden rush of heat course through me, leaving me sweaty and as nervous as a cat. What could I do? I'd already made my argument. He wanted to leave me. I was going to be a divorcée. There would be gossip and stares. I could hear the old hens clucking about it now. *Delphia Barnes left by her war hero husband. What did she do to make him leave? Did she kick him out simply because he no longer had part of his leg? What a terrible girl. She always was, you know.*

"I'm sorry, Delphia. But someday you'll see this was for the best."

I got up then, without another word, and went upstairs to dress and fix my hair. If this was what he wanted, I was going to have to find a way to move on. I did the only thing in the moment I could think to do. I called my mother.

MY SISTERS all rallied around me later that morning. Mama had called and told them what had happened and asked if they would come for lunch at the big house to comfort me. They did, canceling whatever plans they'd had that day. I'd always have my sisters, I thought tearfully.

All of my life, I'd been the feistiest of us. Even more so than Cymbeline, who was her own person without caring what others thought of her. She had a sweetness to her that no amount of ambition could squelch. Over the years, with Viktor by her side, she'd mellowed. She didn't have the edge I had. I was quick and competitive like her but only with my mind rather than my body. I didn't put up with guff from anyone. In fact, mostly I was the one coming up with ways to get everyone mad at me. As a kid, I'd always had good intentions, but often things went the wrong way. Usually, it hadn't taken me long to brush off the dust of defeat and move on to the next project.

But that morning, I was broken. The only man I could ever imagine spending my life with was leaving me. We'd had such little time before he left. If we'd been married longer, perhaps his feelings would be different.

I could do nothing but weep.

I was sitting between Addie and Fiona, who were taking turns patting my knee or shoulder or putting their arms around me. Josephine and Mama sat opposite on the other couch, looking pale and worried. Mama had her hanky out and was twisting and untwisting it as if her life depended on it. Fiona, who smelled of cherries and cookies, wore an attractive purple rayon dress with a flared skirt. Addie, who had been in the middle of one of her writing binges, had come to the house wearing a plaid shirt that belonged to James over a pair of wool trousers and thick socks. "Sorry about my writing uniform," she'd informed us all when she arrived, as if we hadn't seen her this way before. With James gone, she'd been writing for hours every day. She wouldn't tell us the plot of her new novel, saying it would stifle her creativity if she spoke out loud about it.

Cym, on the other hand, was prowling around the sitting room like a panther ready to pounce on his dinner. "This is unbelievable. I would not have thought someone with Jack's strength of character would do such a thing." She wore a pair of riding trousers, brown boots, and a black sweater, having come from a morning ride with Viktor. When Mama called, she'd come straight over instead of changing. Even in my distressed state, I couldn't help but notice how beautiful and strong she was.

Josephine got up to stand in front of the fire, her countenance one of concern but clearly wishing to solve the problem using her intellect. She was dressed in a smart tweed suit, having planned to go into the library this morning before being called out to rescue me. Although she would be called middle-aged by some, she had kept her slender figure and had always worn her sun hat, leaving her fair skin virtually unlined. She'd recently told me how horrific it was to see another war tearing apart families. Today, experiencing what I had with Jack, I understood what she meant more than I ever had before.

"I feel terrible for Jack, even though he's treating you poorly," Jo said. "The horrors of the war followed him home, not to mention losing such a vital part of his manhood."

"You have a unique perspective, darling." Our newest member of the family, an orange tabby cat named Tommy, jumped onto Mama's lap and curled into a happy ball.

"Yes, I believe I do. Phillip still has nightmares," Jo said. "After all these years, at least once a month, he wakes up shouting or thrashing about, mumbling in his sleep. I don't think we can ever understand what it is they've seen or had to do. It never leaves, even if they seem to go on to live ordinary, normal lives."

I nodded, still miserable but having stopped crying. "I don't know how to reach him."

"Give him time, perhaps?" Mama asked. "Let him move home for a while, and you continue living your life, working and tending your garden and home. Maybe it will turn him around to see you steadfast in your love for him."

"Yes, I think that's the right thing to do," Fiona said. "If he knows you'll never give up on him, even with everything that's happened, it may wake him up and see that he belongs with you."

"I don't know if I can live there without him," I said. "Every detail of the house was with him in mind. Even though he's never lived there, it feels as if he's in every room.

Cymbeline stopped in the middle of her pacing. "He needs to feel like he's still a man—one worthy of being with you."

"Yes, I think so, too," Addie said. "But how can anyone but himself convince him that's so?"

"I have an idea," Cym said. "Do you remember how Viktor had me training for my first competition? All the exercises and everything?"

"Yes, I remember." Viktor had her picking up large rocks and doing push-ups and running sprints.

"It was genius," Jo said. "And just what you needed."

"Right." Cym's eyes sparkled, obviously excited over her idea. "What if I go out there and convince him that he can do all of the things he used to do? Get him strong and feeling invincible?"

"But can he do everything he did before?" Mama asked. "It's true that he's not the same. Isn't accepting limitations more realistic?"

"Mama, I'm amazed to hear you say such a thing," Fiona said. "You've always taught us that we can do anything we truly have a passion for, even if we have to work harder than everyone else. Even if it seems impossible to others."

"You were a teacher, Mama," Addie said. "Like James, you believe people can learn new things. That no child should be denied education, no matter their background. Isn't that true in this situation too?"

Mama smiled in her gentle way, her brown eyes warm and loving. "I suppose you're right. I do believe that everyone can learn and improve. However, only if they want to. Motivation is perhaps the problem here. He's despairing, thinking his life's over."

"He counted off all the things he could no longer do," I said, my stomach clenching at the memory. "Horseback riding, swimming, dancing."

"But couldn't he do those things still?" Cym asked. "Maybe not dancing—that one could be tricky, what with crutches and everything."

"Not if he had a prosthetic," Jo said. "Has he said anything about it, Delphia? They improved them after the first war when a lot of men came home just as Jack is."

A spasm of pain shot through me, remembering his face last night in the lamplight, gray and washed out with eyes that looked up at me with defeat and anger. "He said he doesn't want one."

"Ridiculous," Cym said. "He should at least try."

"He says they hurt because they don't fit right," I said.

"Interesting." Now it was Jo's turn to pace. "What if Phillip could design something? He's a master with wood, and he's been checking all these engineering books out of the library. He wants to learn how to make a chair that reclines. It's a hobby. You know how he is—woodworking and design relax him."

"I'll suggest it to Jack," Cym said. "When I find him later and give him a good talking to."

"I don't know if that's a good idea." My stomach fluttered with nerves. "What if he's mad I talked to you all about it?"

"Well, that would hardly be fair," Fiona said. "Since he's told you he wants a divorce. That's something the whole town will know soon enough. If he's worried about people not knowing his business, perhaps he should think about that."

We all stared at her. Fiona was not one for outbursts, especially angry ones.

"And anyway, the man made it home," Fiona said, continuing in the same exasperated tone. "We don't know if the other members of our family will be so lucky, He should count his blessings and have gratitude for being alive."

"That may be so, but right now, he's lost and frightened,"

Mama said. "If he chooses to leave the marriage, then you'll have to accept it. However, until he makes that decision, he is your husband. Which means you must support him as best you can."

"But how?" I asked. How could I do that when he wanted to leave me?

"By trying everything we can to help him," Mama said. "As a family."

JACK

After Delphia left, the phone rang. It was my mother, asking how I was doing and could she stop by to see me? I told her I'd like that very much. Good timing, I'd thought after I hung up. I'd pack what I could and be ready for her to take me home.

I was in the sitting room when she knocked on the door. Instead of getting up, I called to her, telling her to come inside.

She appeared, carrying a box and chattering away without seeming to notice the darkness in the room and my heart. "Hello, honey. Ah, you've shaved. It looks much better. Now we'll take care of that hair of yours. I've brought the rest of your things. I couldn't part with them before you came home, but I promised Delphia to look and see what there was in your room that you might like. We had a pact." She smiled. "As soon as you came home, I'd bring it all over. So here I am." She looked behind her. "Where's Delphia? I smell bacon. She was so excited to cook for you. Did you enjoy your dinner last night?"

"Yes, they were both good."

She set the box back into the hallway. "We can worry about

that later. How are you feeling today?" She asked the question as if I were only recovering from a cold.

"Mama, I want to come home."

Her brow wrinkled. "For dinner? Of course. I missed our family dinners very much."

"No, I mean for good. I'm divorcing Delphia."

She stared at me for what felt like an hour but was really only a few seconds. A myriad of emotions passed across her face —confusion followed by sadness followed by impatience. "Don't be ridiculous. You have no cause for divorce."

"I do, though. Things have changed. I no longer love her." I braced, hoping God didn't strike me dead for lying.

"Of course you do. You've loved her your entire life. I know. I was there for it all."

"Well, I've changed. I'm coming back to live with you. I'll figure out some way to contribute. I've no idea what I'm useful for around the farm. Can't even clean the stalls."

She raised one eyebrow, then crossed her arms over her chest, glaring at me. "Listen to me, young man. You will do no such thing. You made a vow to the woman you loved—the woman who has worked tirelessly to prepare a beautiful home to return to. And you want to run away like a little boy? I don't think so. You stay right here and you figure out how to be the husband she deserves. Anyway, I don't think for one minute you don't love her. You men and your pride."

I started to speak, but she put her hand up. "I don't want to hear whatever sorry excuse you have or how much you pity yourself. You will not divorce Delphia. You will stay here and make this work. And yes, you best find a way to contribute to this marriage and your family instead of moping around here, thinking your world's ended."

"It has," I roared. "Look at me. I can't stand without crutches. I can't even get in a bathtub."

"That's not true. You may not be able to now, but once you

build your strength back up, you'll be able to do most of what you did before. Get those muscles back. You need them more than ever right now. And as far as that goes, why haven't you used your prosthetic leg? The marine doctors must have sent one home with you."

It was my turn to gape at her. "What are you talking about? They didn't send me home with anything."

"They should have. But never mind. We'll see about getting one for you."

"I don't want it."

"Why?"

"Because they're awkward and useless. Like me."

"For God's sake, Jack. You're behaving like a baby. You better get yourself together, and I don't mean tomorrow. I mean today. You hurt Delphia terribly yesterday, that much was obvious. I raised you better than that. Now, I'm leaving and I don't want to hear from you again until you have a plan for how you're going to rebuild her trust and your life."

With that, she turned on her heel and walked out of the room and out the door. I jumped when she slammed the door louder than I'd ever heard her do anything in my life.

AFTER SHOWERING in the new walk-in, I spent the rest of the day moping around and taking intermittent naps on the couch, exhausted by the truth. There was no place to go. My parents wouldn't have me. I had no money to buy a place of my own. The boardinghouse in town had long ago become an inn. Rooms there were way over my price range. They wouldn't have a walk-in shower, either.

That shower. Delphia had managed to have it installed in time for my return. How had she done it? How had she done any of this? She was the most phenomenal woman I'd ever known. Nothing would ever change that.

Still, I had no job and no future. Because of my mother's lack of empathy, I was being forced to live here with the woman I wanted least of all to see what I'd become, skinny and without a limb and as angry as a grizzly bear.

By lunchtime, I'd gotten up to make myself something to eat. I ate cold roast beef leaning against the sink and propping myself up on one crutch. A car in the driveway caught my attention shortly thereafter. It would be Delphia home. Where had she been, anyway? I didn't know her routines. She'd been busy with work and volunteering and learning how to cook, but that's about all I knew.

Irritated by the subsequent knocking at the door, I clumped my way down the hallway. Cymbeline and Fiona stood there, both looking angrier than my mother. This would not end well for me.

"Jack, welcome home," Fiona said, smiling sweetly despite the fire in her eyes. She really was the kindest, gentlest woman. I immediately felt bad for my irritation, followed almost as quickly with dread. Why were they here? Had my wife already told her family? Of course, she had. They were tight, especially the sisters.

"It's good to see you, Jack," Cym said. "May we come inside?"

"I'm busy at the moment." I barricaded the doorway with my large frame.

"We're family, Jack. At least for now. We're coming in." Cym stepped close enough for me to catch a whiff of her musky perfume. One wouldn't think a small woman could have such a threatening presence, but this was Cymbeline Barnes. She was impossible to disobey. How did her children and husband ever rebel against her? They probably didn't. In this way, she was very much like my wife. I'd faced death and horrific tragedy many times in the last year, but I was still afraid of the Barnes sisters.

"Sure, and thanks." I backed away from the doorway to let them pass by and then followed them into the sitting room. With swift, efficient movements, the ladies disposed of their hats and coats, laying them on the back of the couch. I was rude not to take them and hang them in the closet, but it was too much. I could only stand there, leaning into my crutches to wait for whatever lambasting was about to be unleashed upon me.

"Where's Delphia?" Cymbeline asked.

"I don't know," I said.

"May we sit?" Fiona asked.

I nodded my consent, then lumbered over to lower myself onto one of the easy chairs. Or rather, I plummeted to the cushion about as graceful as a baby just learning to walk.

"Delphia told us you want to…move back to your parents," Fiona said.

"We can't even say the word," Cym said, looking down her small nose at me before sitting on the sofa. "Because it's so ludicrous."

I didn't say anything, examining the floor and being careful not to allow any movement in my facial muscles. They could not know how wretched I truly was.

"I suppose you think it's best for her?" Cym asked.

"That's right." I lifted my gaze to meet her eyes. "You can't tell me any different. I know the truth. She's loyal and good and will stay out of duty. I can't have her wreck her life just because mine is. We were married for such a short time. There's no reason we can't annul it and move forward."

"That's not what she wants," Fiona said. "If you were feeling better, you would be able to see that she only cares that you're home. We all have wounds, you know. There's not a person in the world who hasn't suffered or carried some kind of burden. The only thing we must cling to is our family and those we love and who love us. Nothing else can be trusted. Not even our misguided attempts at protecting those we care for. She's a grown woman, capable of making her own decisions."

"That's right. As a matter of fact," Cym said, leaning forward, her forehead pinched with tension, "you're disrespecting her by insisting you know what's best for her. I thought you'd have known that by now, after spending most of your life with her. She is not a woman who needs a man to take care of her. She's perfectly able to do that herself. And she certainly doesn't need you to decide what she wants."

"Do you still love her?" Fiona asked, her eyes wide.

"Tell us the truth," Cym said. "If you can honestly say you don't, then we'll leave here and let it be."

I studied my hands. Reddened and still chapped from the months outdoors, I could hardly recognize them. To think I used to believe I was tough. I had no idea what that meant.

"Jack Depaul, tell us the truth," Fiona said.

I looked up at them, from Fiona to Cym and then back to my hands. "I've loved Delphia all my life. That's the only thing about me that hasn't changed."

"I knew it." Cym stood and stormed over to the fireplace. She tossed several logs onto the embers. They almost immediately caught fire, shedding orange light into the room. Outside, the afternoon was dim. We'd get more snow soon.

How I'd missed the changing hues of the sky and scents of the forest. Not any forest, this particular one. My home.

"Have you told your parents about your wish to move home?" Fiona asked.

I nodded, flushing with embarrassment. "My mother just left, actually."

"And?" Cym continued to glare at me, reminding me of her little sister.

"She's having none of it," I said, letting out a sigh of defeat. "I've no place to go." My eyes stung. I fought the tears that

163

wanted to come. These were women I'd known since my first memories. The sisters of my beloved. Lying to them was fruitless, yet I couldn't loosen my resolve. I must remember that it was Delphia's happiness that mattered most, not mine. It was too late for me.

Cym appeared to have little sympathy for me. "Are you really going to sit here and tell me you have no place to go when your wife spent every minute and dollar she had to make a home for you to return to? You should be ashamed of yourself. Your parents raised you better than to sit around and wallow in self-pity. You get yourself up and dust yourself off, like any good horseman would do, and come up with the plan for the rest of your life. The rest of your *married* life."

"You don't understand," I said. "What this is like."

"You're correct," Fiona said softly. "We don't. But we do know that between our two families, there has always been love and respect. The joining of our families by marriage is sacred to all of us. Including you. I know it is. You're hurting and sad and angry. We understand this, at least. We also know that the best thing you could do is to let Delphia back into your heart. She will be by your side through whatever comes."

"I don't want her beholden to the vows we made," I said. "Not now when I'm no longer the man she married."

"She promised you she would love you through sickness and health," Cym said. "Not out of duty but from great love. That's not changed. It will never change, even if you try with all your might to push her away."

Fiona stood, reaching for her coat. "We'll let you be now. We're sorry for being interfering, but that's the way we do things in our family." She touched my shoulder and looked into my eyes. "I *am* sorry for what's happened to you. I'm sure it will be a period of adjustment as you get used to the way it is now, but you came home, Jack. My boys are still over there, and I don't know if I'll ever see either one of them again." Her eyes flooded, and she pressed a handkerchief to her mouth for a second before continuing. "You remember that, all right? You have come home. Changed, yes, but home just the same. Make the most of your life. You're alive and should be happy for it."

Deeply ashamed, I hung my head. She was right. I should be grateful, but all I could feel was anger. Could someone as angry as I ever love anyone properly again? I was a mass of darkness, and my wife was the opposite. "She deserves better than me."

"You're darn right she does," Cym said, snappish. "The way you're acting right now, she most certainly deserves someone better. But you're that man, under all this self-pity. You're still the man she married."

"I'm not," I said.

"If I weren't a lady, I'd curse at you right now," Cym said. "Instead, I'm going to leave here and expect that the next time I see you, the Jack we know and love will have emerged. You can do this. You *must* do this. If not, you'll have broken the heart of the woman you claim to love. That is the worst thing you could ever do to her, so if you truly do love her, then it's time for you to make this right. Be the man we know you are."

Cym flung her coat over one arm, apparently too warm from her tirade to put it on despite the snow that had begun to fall outside the windows. "I'll expect to see you at Sunday dinner, but before that, I'll be around to begin our training program."

"What did you say?" I blinked, looking up at her. "Training program?"

"Regimen, perhaps, would be a better name for what I have planned for you." Cym picked up her red felt hat. Instead of pinning it back into place, she let it dangle in her hand.

"Regimen? I'm no longer a marine," I said. "And have you noticed I'm missing a leg?" I inwardly cringed at my rudeness but couldn't seem to squelch it. The bitterness had overtaken every part of me, even the manners my mother had taught me.

"Which is why you need to get stronger than ever," Cym

said. "Viktor and I will come up with a plan for you to rebuild your strength in your upper body and your leg. The more muscle you have, the better your balance will be."

"Jo mentioned that Phillip might be able to design a prosthetic for you," Fiona said. "He's clever that way, you know."

"I don't want that," I said.

"You might," Cym said. "Especially if it fit well and didn't cause you any pain."

"No," I said, raising one of my crutches. "These are my legs now."

"Give it a chance," Fiona said. "Please, Jack? For Delphia? Can't you find a way to fight for her?"

"I don't know." My voice shook. "I don't know if I'm strong enough to see a future for myself."

"You are," Cym said. "You'll see."

Fiona leaned over and kissed me on the cheek. "Come into town and get a haircut at the shop. Everyone wants to welcome you home. You're a hero, Jack. Don't forget that part."

I didn't get up when they walked out of the room and out the front door. Instead, I remained in the chair, a broken, crumpled excuse for a man, and watched the fire slowly die.

166

18

DELPHIA

I spent most of the day at my office at the back of the club. We'd decided to open it once more for a few nights a week only. The days would continue to be devoted to war efforts but in the evenings, we would welcome anyone who wanted a respite from the dreariness of life. My job now was to come up with a schedule for the staff, hire a new bartender, and negotiate a contract with a new gin supplier. By the time I looked up from my work, night had fallen. A quick glance at the clock told me it was time for me to head home. My stomach growled, as if to remind me that it was suppertime. Often, I ate upstairs in the kitchen of the lodge's dining room since it was lonely to go home to a cold and empty house. I'd thought Jack's return home would change all that, but I doubted he would be there by the time I arrived home.

Still, I tidied my desk and put on my coat and gloves and went out to my car. I'd told Jack it was time to get on with it. The same could be said for me. I had to face whatever came.

Driving home, I took my time. About three inches of snow had fallen that afternoon, but now it was clear and cold, which made the roads slick. By the time I turned into the driveway toward my house, fatigue overwhelmed me. I should go to my parents for dinner instead of facing the evening alone, but I didn't know if I had the strength to carry on polite conversation when every ounce of me ached. While I'd concentrated on tasks at the office, I'd been able to shove aside my heartbreak. Or, at the very least, distract myself with work so the piercing pain faded somewhat.

Now, however, it all came rushing back to me. Fighting tears, I drove into our detached garage and turned off the car. For a moment, I sat and stared out the front window with my hands still gripping the steering wheel. I must go in and greet this new form of loneliness. All these months while Jack was away, I'd been able to keep myself together because I had hope. Everything was about preparing for his return. I'd never imagined that he would be here and yet further away than he'd ever been.

I pulled my coat closed and made my way to the house. In my heels, the cold crept up my skirt. I'd need to start a fire right away. The idea of sitting in front of it, eating a piece of bread and butter as I'd done many nights before, made me start to cry all over again. I'd become accustomed to crying over the last few days. The dampness almost felt like a salve to my dry, pained eyes.

It was when I was nearing the back door that I realized the scent of smoke filled the air. I looked up to see it coming from the brick chimney. Had my father come by to make a fire for me? The idea of that made me tear up again. It was with blurry vision that I opened the door to my kitchen. The lights were on, and it was not as cold as it normally was when I got home. My father must have left the lights on and stoked the fire in anticipation of my return from work.

However, that was not the case. Jack stood at the sink, propped up by his crutches. I blinked at the sight of him. He'd had a haircut and with his shaved face, he looked almost like the man I'd said goodbye to all those months ago. His cheeks were thinner, and his eyes were dull, but he seemed more like himself.

"I thought you'd be gone by now." I clutched my handbag to my chest. My toes were cold from walking through the few inches of snow. Normally, I took them off first thing and put on a pair of slippers I kept near the door.

"Yes, well, it seems I have no place to go. My mother refused to let me come home."

I stared at him. "She did?" My mood lifted slightly. Was it possible that he would see that it was here with me that he belonged? Had his mother been able to shift his thoughts some-what? Even if it were only a slight nudge, it might help us move closer together.

"Yes. And then, to further add to my wonderful day, your sisters came by."

"Which ones?"

"Cym and Fiona."

"I would have thought it would be Jo and Cym," I said under my breath. They were the bossy ones. "What did my sisters want?"

"Cym wants to torture me through a process to improve my strength. Fiona kindly reminded me that I was alive and there was no guarantee Bleu and Beaumont would return and that I should be grateful and make the best of things. In addition, Phillip thinks he can design a prosthetic for me."

I bit the inside of my lip, unsure what to say. My sisters were right to suggest these things, but I was fairly certain my husband didn't agree.

"They said it would be worse for you if we divorced than if you remained my faithful wife." His lips twitched into a mirth-less grin, making him appear like an evil character in a play for a moment. He was not evil, I reminded myself, simply hurt and angry.

I nodded. "That's true. I don't want this. You know that."

"But what if you're wrong? What if we get a few months into all this and you realize what a burden I am? Or you cannot look at me now that I'm hideous?"

"You're not hideous." I smiled. "Especially now that you've gotten a shave and haircut."

Sighing, he hung his head. His newly shorn hair, longer on top than the sides, fell over his forehead. "You'll see. Once I show you what my stump looks like, you'll run away fast."

"Try me." I lifted my chin, defiant. Truthfully, I was frightened to see what they'd done to him. Would it disgust me? I couldn't imagine anything about my husband ever having that effect, but maybe he was right. Would I no longer want to lie beside him in our marital bed? What if my reaction hurt him further and proved that he was right?

"I don't think that's a good idea," Jack said flatly.

"We'll never know unless we try, will we?" I spoke with much more bravado than I felt. *Be courageous*, I told myself. *He deserves the best from you, not some childish reaction.*

"It's disgusting. You'll see."

"Fine. Let's go upstairs. You can show it to me in our bedroom."

His eyes glittered as he seemed to contemplate this idea. Finally, he nodded. "Yes, let's get it over with. The sooner the better. Perhaps my mother will take me in once you run away."

"I'm not a scared bunny rabbit."

For the first time since he'd come home, he laughed. Not his hearty, lighthearted chortle from before but more of a bitter cackle. I suddenly knew then that it would be easier to see his stump than hear the transformation of his laugh.

I turned and headed toward the stairs, not stopping when I came to the hallway, even though I was uncertain he was following. When I reached the second floor, I heard the thumping of his crutches. I went into my bedroom to wait for him.

I sat on the chair near the window and waited. Thoughts and images from our honeymoon days played before me like a series of paintings. We'd been so in love and so infatuated with each other's mouths and faces and bodies. My legs had been entangled with his and the sheets and blankets as we drifted off to sleep that first night. I'd never been as happy as I'd been in that moment. How naive I'd been to think that our whole lives were ahead of us. That nothing could come between us.

He entered the room, shutting the door behind him with a swift push of one of his crutches. He was really quite adept with those things. Soon, he would be even more so. If he would train with Cym and Viktor, he could become strong again. His shoulders and arms would widen with muscles as they once had. If only he would try.

I held my breath as he crossed the room to sit on one side of the bed. He set aside his crutches and lay back on the bed to unbuckle his belt. Two holes in from what they'd been before, I noticed.

"Turn around," he said. "I don't want you to watch me undress."

I did as he asked, listening to the sounds of the bed creaking under his weight and the thump of something metal hitting the floor. The belt buckle?

"Okay, you can look now."

I turned slowly, holding my breath and silently praying to God to guide me to react the right way. *Please, don't let me hurt him by my reaction.*

He stood on his one leg with the crutches under each arm, wearing white shorts and an undershirt. I remembered them from our honeymoon. He'd written to me while he was overseas that they'd issued shorts and undershirts in tan to keep them from attracting enemy fire while they were drying on the line.

He was too thin—that was the first thing I noticed. His stomach was nearly concave. Gone were the chest and arm muscles that my hands had loved traveling over and memorizing. I lowered my gaze to his legs. The right one was a stump just above the knee. Even in the dim light of the room, I could see the skinny scars where they'd sewn his skin together. I steadied myself by leaning against the arm of a chair. It *was* hard to see. I couldn't lie to myself or him about that. My poor man had suffered so much. The impact of what he'd truly gone through coursed through my veins and made me dizzy. "Oh, Jack, I'm sorry. I'm so sorry this happened to you."

"I told you. I'm a monster." His mouth tightened, and a muscle in his face pulsed. I'd not been able to see how thin his face had become before he shaved. Now it seemed as if the skin clung to bone instead of flesh.

"You're not," I said. "You're still Jack."

"No, don't make excuses. I can see what you think of me." His voice trembled, but it was less angry than I'd heard him since he'd come home. Not so terse. More like himself.

"What do I think then, if you're so sure?" I asked, angry.

"I saw you lean against the chair for support," he said. "My grotesque leg—*stump*—made you dizzy and light-headed."

"I'll not lie and say it isn't hard to see what they did to you. However, I'm not faint from disgust but from the truth of what happened to you. Yes, it's right there in front of me now. I see the scars and the space where your leg once held you up tall and proud." I looked up at his handsome face. He was not a monster. He was still my Jack. There may have been less of him but he was still there, as beautiful to me as he'd ever been. "You are still the most beautiful thing in this world to me, Jack Depaul."

"But how can I be?" His voice grew soft in the quiet room.

"Did I ever tell you how I get goosebumps anytime I'm close to you?"

He shook his head. "Can't say I recall that."

"I did. I do. Little prickles that run up and down my entire body. When we were younger, I could feel when you walked into a room, even if I was on the other side of it. The first time we ever danced together, I had a feeling I'd never felt before, this longing to be closer to you. To have you so close that we would meld into one. Then we kissed, and all the daydreams I'd had were proved ridiculous—for it was so much better than I could have ever imagined. The way my skin and my body burned under your touch? Nothing prepared me for the sheer pleasure you gave me. Those nights of our honeymoon? They're all I could think of for so long."

"And now I look like this. The idea of how disgusting I must seem to you hurts worse than any of the rest of it." He tilted his head. A teardrop traveled down his face. I moved toward him, inching slowly so as not to spook him.

When I reached him, I spread a hand over his cheek, absorbing his tears into my own skin. "You're not disgusting to me. You're you. The most handsome man I ever met. The cleverest and sweetest and the only one who could make me laugh so hard it made my stomach hurt. And do you know what?"

"What?" His eyes closed. It was slight, but I could feel that he leaned a little into my hand, as if he head had suddenly become heavy.

"You're still you. All those things are still true. You give me goosebumps and heart flutters and a naughty feeling in my lady parts."

That made him chuckle, even as more tears slid down his face.

"I want you back. *You*, not some idea you had of yourself, but the real you. Part of your leg is gone. Is it as pretty as the other one now? No, it's not. But you're as beautiful to me as you ever were. Nothing could ever change how you make me feel or how much I long to be with you. Do you understand?"

"I don't. I don't understand." His shoulders pitched forward.

I wrapped my arms around his neck. "Darling, I'm here. I'm always going to be here, even if you try to push me away, even if you walk out the door and never look back to see that I wait for you. I'll be waiting for you with the lights on, just as I have all the months you were away."

A spasm shuddered through him. He buried his face into my neck. "I've missed you so," he whispered. "Every minute of every day."

"Then let me love you the way God made me to do. Together, we can weather this storm and any others that come our way."

For a few seconds, we remained close, with my arms around his neck and my slim frame pressed against him. His arms remained supported by his crutches, I realized. He would not be able to embrace me fully ever again. The truth of that took my breath away. I'd been thinking of it too much from my own perspective. This loss of a limb was so much more than that. It was a death in a way, a change so profound that it affected every single part of his life. Our life.

He pulled away to look down at me. "You're so beautiful. Even more so than when I left. How is that possible?"

"I don't think it is." I smiled and brought one hand to rest just above the collar of his shirt. "The war has been hard on us all, but this—this thing that's happened to you—it's happened to me too. I'm your wife, Jack. I feel the loss too."

"What do you mean?" His eyes and expression had softened. He almost looked like my Jack, but there was still a wariness, an uncertainty about which direction to go. Stay or leave.

"I mean that I'm sad. You won't be able to twirl me around the dance floor or hold me tightly. The crutches will always be in the way. I'm grieving the old ways too. Don't think you're alone in that."

"What else will you miss?" His voice sounded hoarse in the quiet room.

"Watching you chop wood. Or ride a horse." Even as I said them, I knew there were ways, if we were inventive, that he could get close to doing these again. We had to be creative. Yet I had an instinct to keep going. Jack Depaul was never one to run from a challenge. Would that spark his competitive nature? I needed him to rebel against his circumstance. To prove that he could still conquer this life, even with the blows he'd endured. "Carrying our baby in your arms. Lifting her or him out of their bed when they're scared. Skiing." That one hadn't occurred to me until just now. I had an image of him flying down our mountain, his red scarf trailing behind him. He'd been so alive and virile. It was true, I'd been drawn to that part of him, and he was no longer the same. Yet I could still see the potential in him, regardless of his physical capabilities, to do whatever he wished. He was still a man. A hero, to me and the rest of the country. He could overcome this. I knew he could.

"What else?" Jack asked.

"Swimming in the creek or river. Chasing me across the meadow. Lifting me up and spinning me around."

His eyes closed again. "Yes, I'll miss all those too." Tears slid from his closed lids, soaking his face and dribbling into the collar of his shirt. "I want my old life back."

"We can miss all of those things together." I brushed his damp face with the backs of my fingers. "If you'd let me in, we could grieve together. And then, after we've let ourselves mourn the life we thought we would have, we can figure out the plan for the future."

His voice shook as the words spilled from him. "I've been so proud. I realize that now. Of being the strongest and bravest. I no longer have either of those attributes. I'm weak and broken, perhaps beyond repair. I might never be the man I was, Delphia. The man you fell in love with."

"We've both changed since the day we married. That's what the war has done. However, every couple changes throughout the course of their marriages. Our changes were forced upon us quickly, I can admit that. But we're still us. Jack and Delphia, best friends, just as we've always been."

"You can really imagine a life with me now? A life with a man who can no longer swing you around the dance floor—" He stopped as sobs overcame him. His chest heaved with the obvious effort to stop crying.

"I can imagine that life. In fact, we're in it right now." I stroked his back. "Please, darling, let me in. Stay with me. Take me to bed."

He lifted his head and blinked, his expression credulous. "Now?"

My lip trembled. Why had I said it? Just to be rejected? "I know. It's scandalous before dinner." I spoke lightly, but the tears in my voice came through anyway.

He shook his head. "It has nothing to do with the time of day. How can you want to be with me? I'm deformed and grotesque. You've seen it for yourself. Anyway, I have no interest in that. Or you. If I had anywhere left to go, I would."

The pain of his words was a combination of a punch in the stomach and the wind being knocked out of me. It was my second time to stare at him in disbelief. How could the boy I loved ever speak to me this way? He was right. I was disgusted by him, not because of any physical deformity but because he was cruel and selfish. I'd poured my heart out to him, and he came back with this?

I backed away from him, leaving him to stand alone by the bed. "Go then. Get out of my house." My voice shook with rage and hurt and everything in between. "If you don't want to be here in the home I made for us, then just go. I've no use for someone who would rather wallow in self-pity than make a new life for himself with the woman who so desperately loves him."

Without meeting his gaze—for all I knew he wasn't looking at me anyway—my chest aching so much I could hardly breathe, I headed for the door. He didn't want me that way any longer. Or was it that he could no longer think of intimacy? Either way, it was not a marriage. Not the kind I wanted. Was he right? Was he too broken for us to try again?

For the first time, I started to believe he was right.

19

JACK

What was I supposed to do now? I'd successfully made her angry enough that she wanted me to leave. However, I had no place to go. My mother and father didn't want me. My wife's family would soon grow to hate me. Henry, who would have taken me in even though I was behaving like a boorish pig, was overseas. Possibly dead already for all I knew.

After Delphia walked away, I dressed and went across the hallway to the other room. She'd had window seats installed, an homage to the bedroom she'd had as a child. Now, I sank into one and slumped against the wall. I'd not thought it possible to hate myself as much as I did now. The look in her eyes when I'd said I didn't want her anymore had broken my heart into a thousand pieces. I would never be able to forgive myself for hurting her, yet I knew it was for the best. I'd seen her expression when she saw my stump for the first time. I knew her. All my life, I'd been studying her and memorizing what each nuanced tone of her voice and expression on her face meant. She'd been shocked and dismayed and disgusted. Whatever words came from her mouth, they were lies.

Here I'd thought she was a rebel when it turned out she was a nice girl like her sisters. One who would never turn their back on their family or husbands or children, even when they should.

I'd go to my parents' tomorrow. They'd have to take me in if I showed up on the doorstep with my suitcase. Turning away their own son would not be something they could do, even if they were angered by my actions.

I should have been hungry for an evening meal, but the discussion with Delphia had worn me out. I collapsed onto one of the narrow beds and stared up at the ceiling.

I fell asleep. When I woke later, the house was quiet and dark. I got up, bed creaking, and went to the window. Peering into the darkness, I could see only that it had snowed a great deal while I was asleep. Had Delphia gone out in this? There was no way to see if there were tire tracks into the garage. What if she had driven out to see her parents and gotten stuck in the snowstorm? No, she wouldn't have done that. She was a Colorado girl. She knew when to drive and when to stay home.

I went into the bathroom to use the toilet and brush my teeth. My stomach growled with hunger. Should I go downstairs and see if there was anything to eat? I'd make so much noise going down the stairs. Hunger won out in the end.

As quietly as possible, which wasn't really, I climbed down the stairs to the first floor and then headed toward the kitchen. A noise from the living room distracted me from my journey. I hobbled over to see Delphia curled up in a chair near the fireplace, wearing a robe over flannel pajamas. Were those mine? They were. She slept in my old pajamas? Logs burned orange in the hearth, the only light in the dark room. She didn't turn as I approached. She had her hair unpinned, and it hung about her shoulders in loose waves. Her fair skin had a moonlike quality. Longing for her overwhelmed me. I loved her so much I thought I might die from it. I took in deep breaths to try to steady myself.

179

"You're still here," she said flatly.

"Yes, I'll go in the morning. I fell asleep."

"There's no dinner if that's what you're looking for." Her voice was cold and distant, as if I were a stranger. Perhaps I was.

"I'll find something. Some bread or whatever there is."

"Fine." She reached out to the table next to her and picked up a glass with amber liquid. Whiskey or brandy? That wasn't like her. It was nearing midnight. I'd never known her to drink much. But from the half-empty bottle over on the bar, it looked as if she'd had more than one. Or had she been drinking the whole time I was away? Had she been unable to sleep, worried about me, and come down some nights to warm herself with a drink?

You don't get to care. You don't get to ask about her habits. You sent her away.

I asked anyway.

"Since when do you drink?"

"Special occasions," she said. "Like the night your husband tells you he's leaving. You know, events such as this need a drink or two."

I stood, leaning into my crutches, unable to think of a retort. Nothing biting came to mind, as it had earlier. Instead, I wanted to sit next to her and pull her onto my lap and kiss her until she forgot every stupid thing I'd said to her.

"Or when the telegram comes that your sister's child's been killed in action on the Western Front."

"What?" I lurched and my stomach knotted. "Who?"

"Bleu. She found out just after suppertime. My mother called to tell me."

"Oh, God." I sank into the other leather chair, afraid I might be sick. Bleu gone? It was impossible to comprehend that a man with his spirit and good heart could be gone. His dark eyes and wide smile played before me. "The four of us…" I didn't finish the sentence. It was stupid to do so. She knew how close the four of us had been in high school. Fiona, I thought. And Li. They would be devastated.

"Rescued him from the streets of Paris only to lose him on a battleground in France," Delphia said, voice catching. "He deserved so much better."

"They all do."

We sat in silence for a few minutes until the logs shifted. My instinct was to get up and toss another few on the fire, but it would be impossible. As I was thinking this, Delphia got up and did the job for me. This is how it would be all our lives. Her doing the work I should do.

"I'd kill him with my bare hands if I could," Delphia said.

Her viciousness surprised me. I sat up straighter and looked over at her. "Who?"

"Hitler."

"Yes, well, I did my best."

"You gave so much, Jack. I'm sorry. I'm sorry for Bleu. He was such a gentle soul. To think that he was all alone over there. I hope he didn't suffer. I hope he knew how loved he was back home." She started to cry, covering her face with a hanky, her shoulders shaking with grief. Our friend. The sweetest and kindest of all of us. He would not have the chance to fall in love or marry or have children. To see the Colorado sky he'd loved so much. Not ever again.

"I can't go on like this," I said. "The grief and anger are all that I am now."

"And this makes it worse." She'd stopped crying and wiped her eyes and stared into the fire.

My head throbbed. I massaged my temples, trying to make sense of what I'd just been told. Was it the message I needed to stop feeling sorry for myself? As my mother had said, I came home. I lived. Others might not be so lucky. I looked over at my beautiful wife, in pain. How had it come to this? The two of us had been so young and hopeful just a year ago. Now look at us.

"I'm sorry," I said. "I'm sorry for all of it."

She looked over at me, her eyes hard in the glowing firelight. "What are you sorry for? Breaking my heart? Our friend's death? That I can't kill Hitler with my bare hands?"

I barked out a laugh. "It would be nice if you could do that."

She hung her head, gazing into the glass.

"Do you want another one?" I asked.

"I would, but I'm too weary to get up." She dangled the glass from her hand over the side of the chair. Her hand seemed small and her wrist so thin.

I stood and adjusted the crutches in such a way that I could reach for her glass. It was only one leg I was missing, not both. And I was alive. I could get a drink for my wife. "Give it to me. I'll get it."

Her gaze flickered up to my face. "Yeah?"

"Yeah. I'll get one for myself too."

I reached for the glass and put it in the pocket of my trousers, then crossed the few feet over to the chest where she kept the booze. Putting all my weight on my right side, I managed to pour a splash into her glass.

She was behind me by then, so close I could smell her perfume. "Give it here. Pour one for yourself, too, and I'll bring them over to the fire."

"All right." I didn't like it, but what choice did I have?

Once we were back in the chairs before the fire, I took a sip of the liquid fire, which scorched its way down my throat.

"When did you start drinking whiskey?" I asked.

"Tonight."

I chuckled. "I wondered. I couldn't imagine you here drinking by yourself every night."

"It never occurred to me before now. I've been moving too fast, working all the time here at the house or at the lodge or doing my charity work for the war. No time to worry or think about whatever you were facing. That was the plan, anyway."

"Did it work?"

"Not for one moment," she said. "You were always in my thoughts, no matter how busy I kept myself. But tonight is different. Tonight you're home and you've changed so much and you no longer love me. Then I found out dear Bleu was dead, buried someplace in France in an unmarked grave. So I went to the whiskey cabinet and I poured one and sat right here and let myself feel bad."

I sipped my drink, becoming accustomed to the burning sensation. "The house looks beautiful. You did a really good job of it."

"Thank you. I enjoyed it, imagining the whole time what it would be like when you got back. I even thought we'd have babies. Such a fool."

"It wasn't foolish to think so." The pain in my chest was back, crushing me, taking the last of my energy. Holding on. Hating. It was exhausting. "You know I wanted that."

"I learned to cook. That was foolish. Since I'll be living with my folks for the rest of my life. These chairs here? I ordered them especially for us, so we could be like my parents and grow old together by the fire."

I shook my head. Moving back with her parents? No, this wasn't right. "Why wouldn't you stay here?"

She didn't answer for a few seconds, taking another sip of her drink. "It's a strange thing. I've never lived here with you, but it felt as if I had since I did it all for you. Now that you're here but not here and don't want to be married, I cannot bear to stay here."

The alcohol was starting to take effect. I was warm and loose. No pain in my phantom leg. I wanted my wife on my lap. I wanted to hold her and tell her everything was going to be all right. But I didn't know if that was true. What if I was wrong and leaving her wasn't the best thing for either of us? What then?

A crushing weight thundered down upon me and pressed into me at every angle. Walls seemed to close in around me. I might suffocate under the force.

A voice whispered in my ear. Bleu's voice? *Don't let the darkness win, brother.*

Out loud, I said, "I don't know how."

"What?" Delphia peered at me, her brow wrinkled in confusion.

Reach for the light, Bleu whispered. *Reach for your wife.*

"I can't let it win." I downed the rest of my drink and set it on the table between us. Bleu was right. And he was here still, guiding me. The only way to get out from under this boulder or elephant or whatever this heinous thing suffocating me was to reach for the light. Reach for my Delphia. The love of my life. My best friend and companion. The woman who was willing to do whatever it took to make me happy. "I'm so afraid. My love, I'm so afraid."

She leaned forward, setting her drink aside. "Of what? You've already been to hell and back."

"Of ruining your life. Of trapping you in a marriage you wish never happened. To see your love fade little by little or maybe all at once."

"It is not so. It will never be so."

I couldn't stop myself. I reached for her.

"Come here," I said, my hand stretching out over the table between us. "Come to me."

She lifted one eyebrow and watched me with suspicion in her eyes. "Why?"

"Because I want you. I want you to sit with me—so that I can feel your heart beating and smell your hair and...and kiss you." I stretched my hand across the table between us. "If it's true that I don't disgust you now, come to me. Please, Delphia, come be my wife."

She rose to her feet. Her silky dressing gown fell over the old flannel pajamas she wore. What a pair they were, beauty and beast, like us. "You've been so cruel."

"I know. I'm sorry." My voice broke. "It's like this hardness is in me now and I can't find how to get out of it. I love you so much it hurts, and I've been trying to protect you so that you can have the life you deserve."

"My life is you."

"My life is you," I said. "It's always been you."

She looked at me, long and hard. Finally, a shift seemed to come over her, too. A decision to trust me once more. Her expression lost the tautness of earlier, and her shoulders drooped. "Please, don't leave here. Stay with me."

"I'm staying."

"If I come to you, do you promise never to turn me away again? I don't know if I can live through it again. Not now. Not after Bleu and what I'll face tomorrow when I go to Fiona. I'm weak. For the first time in my life, I feel as if I might not be strong enough for this world. Without you, what is the point of anything?"

Tears were leaking from my hot eyes once more. She blurred in front of me as if I were looking out a window obscured by rain. "I can't even bring you a drink."

"Not yet. But I know you. You'll find a way." She knelt by my chair and took my outstretched hand and held it against her cheek. "You smell just the same, like soap and pine needles. My favorite smell in the whole world."

"Honestly, Delphia, I don't know what's best for either of us. But I'm without the strength to leave you. I want to stay with you. It's all I've ever wanted. It was all a lie. I love you more than anything, even myself. I want you to be happy and to have a good life and I can't bear it if you're staying out of pity."

"I stay because I want you, just as I always have."

My crutches were resting side by side against the arm of the chair. I did not need them now, I thought. I can still bring my wife to my lap. I sat up straighter and hauled her off the floor and onto my thighs.

She squeaked, obviously surprised, then looked into my eyes and spoke with such tenderness in her voice that a lump formed in my throat. "Does it hurt? Your leg—with me here like this?"

"No, it doesn't. You feel good. Like medicine. Like nothing is wrong with me."

"Oh, Jack, I've missed you so, and there's nothing wrong with you. You're perfect."

"I've missed you. So much." I kissed her and stroked her hair and murmured in her ear how much I loved her. And we were both crying and kissing all at once. When we took a breath, she stared into my eyes, and the love that radiated from her took my breath away. The elephant that had threatened to crush me under its enormous weight lifted and a light as delicate and filmy as the winter sun filled me instead. "Is it true? Are you still attracted to me? Do you still want to be in my bed?"

"More than anything."

"My wife," I whispered. "I've come home to you at last."

LATER, wrapped together under the covers in the bed she'd so lovingly made for us, we talked, mostly about her and her family and all that I'd missed while I was away. That started us reminiscing about the times we had with Bleu and set us off crying again. This time the tears were more of a salve than the bitter ones of earlier. They dampened my stinging eyes with the salty tears of grief for our dear friend. Finally, as morning light crept through the shades, we slept. She'd not asked me about what happened the day I was hurt, and I was glad. At some point, I would have to tell her. Not yet. Not during these moments of reconciliation when we were fragile and timid, afraid to break the newly formed bonds between us. Anyway, I wanted only to bask in her warmth and love, not conjure up the images of those terrible days.

I woke sometime in the mid-morning. Delphia was still next to me, sleeping curled on her side facing me. I watched her easy breathing and her cheeks flushed from the warmth we made between us and her hair tousled from our lovemaking. I would get stronger. I had to. I must increase my strength with the limbs I had left so that I could make love to my wife. That's all there was to it. I needed to ride a horse again and learn how to dance with a prosthetic and be grateful that I was alive. I'd made it home to my beloved. Now it was time to make good on all the promises I'd made her on our wedding day.

As quietly as I could, I got out of bed and used the crutches to cross the hall to the bathroom. In the shower, I used the fancy soap left by Delphia, and the warmth of the water in the cold room wakened and refreshed me. Today was the day. I would begin my transformation, not to the me of old, for that man had been killed on the battlefield, but to a new version of myself. One with scars and a wound that left nothing but a blank space and a heart newly opened to pain. Yet in a bed across the hallway lay the motivation for change. I must be better, for Delphia and for myself. I was alive when Bleu was not.

In the shower, with Delphia's sweet-smelling soap wafting in the steam, I could almost imagine I was whole. But I was not and wouldn't be, at least not physically. The sooner I accepted that, the better. For it was through acceptance that I would find peace. I bowed my head and prayed for Bleu and all of those who loved him, especially Fiona and Li and his twin brother. Then I said a few words silently to Bleu himself. "May you rest in peace, my friend, in the house of the Lord. I'll see you again someday. Until then, I'll do my best to truly live, so that I might honor your memory."

And his voice came back to me in answer. *I believe in you.*

2 0

DELPHIA

I called over at Cym and Viktor's when I woke sometime
after eleven. I'd never slept as late in my life and filled
with sweaty guilt the moment I sat up in bed, remembering Bleu and my poor sister. There was no answer at her
house, so I called my mother's next. Jasper picked up the phone,
informing me that everyone had gone to Fiona and Li's.

I could hear Jack's movements downstairs in the kitchen.
Already, I was growing accustomed to the sound of his crutches
on the floors. I would bathe and dress before I went down,
knowing I must get to Fiona's to be with the rest of my family.

The bathroom was still steamy. Jack must have showered
already. I did the same, quickly, and then dressed. I smelled
coffee when I descended the stairs. In the kitchen, Jack was
sitting at the table writing in the notebook I kept on the counter
to jot down lists or reminders.

"Good morning," I said suddenly apprehensive. Would last
night prove to be an anomaly? Would the angry, mean Jack
return?

He smiled and closed the notebook. "Darling, did you get
enough rest?"

"I did."

He pushed back from the table and patted his lap. "Come here. Sit with me?"

I went to him and did his bidding, only too happy to oblige.

"I've decided that having you right here is a good substitute for holding you standing up. I can use my arms without the crutches getting in the way."

"I think it's a good solution." Already he looked better, less drawn and thin. I brushed his hair from his forehead and kissed him. "Any regrets about last night?" I had to ask.

"My only regret is that I acted like such an idiot. I'm not saying I won't have moments of self-pity again, but I'm going to do better. I want more than anything to make it up to you and to Bleu."

"I love you so much," I whispered in his ear and held him tightly around the neck, pressing my chin into his thick hair.

"I've been making a list of all the ways I could make Bleu proud of me," Jack said. "Ways to honor him by being the best I can be."

I kissed him. "We can do it together."

THAT AFTERNOON, I sat with my sisters and mother at Fiona's dining room table. We'd made tea and sent it up to Fiona's bedroom, but it had come back untouched. Li was with her, so we knew she would be all right, even though she refused to come down to see us. Her grief had tightened around her in a vicious hold.

As for the rest of my sisters, their children were all at school, so we gathered together, wishing there was something we could do, but knowing there was not. Fiona's precious boy was gone.

I'd just finished telling my sisters and Mama about Jack's transformation the night before. "Bleu's death brought us closer together," I said, fighting tears. "It was as if he sent us a gift from heaven, reminding Jack that he was still here, alive, if not a little crushed. Our sorrow broke Jack open, and he let me back in."

Josephine, who had been knitting away all afternoon, looked up from the wool sock she was making to send to the soldiers. "Poor, sweet Jack. I knew he would come around eventually."

"It took him less time than I thought it would." Cym had been pacing around the dining room, sitting for a moment before springing back up again with nervous energy. "Maybe he'll come train with me after all. I've been thinking of ways to build the strength in his good leg."

"I don't know if he'll want it, but Phillip's made some drawings and plans for a prosthetic leg," Jo said. "He thinks he can make it so it fits him well, lessening the pain of the attachment."

"If anyone can figure it out, it's Phillip," Mama said.

"Thank you all for believing in him," I said. "I have to admit, I'd given up."

Mama, sitting next to me, her cup of tea untouched, patted my knee. "I'm glad, darling, but not surprised. He loves you too much to stop fighting."

Addie floated into the room, bringing a plate of cookies she wouldn't be able to eat because of her problems with flour. Her plain dress was loose against her flat frame. Sometimes I wondered what she ate at all. She'd become so thin since James shipped off. I knew she spent most nights writing, unable to sleep all alone in an empty bed. The smear of ink on her finger and thumb told the story of the words that spilled from the pen. I hoped she would get a good novel out of this hard time since there wasn't much good I could see from this terrible war. We needed stories more than ever. Daily, letters came from readers from all over the country, telling Addie how much her books had helped them during these lonely, frightening months. These correspondences comforted Addie as much as her novels did for those who wrote them.

Addie set the plate in the middle of the table. "These are from Lizzie. She came to the kitchen door just now, not wanting to disturb us. The poor thing had been crying all night and fretting about what she could do to help. You know how much she loves Fiona."

"Dear Lizzie," Mama said. "What would our family do without her?"

Addie sat on the other side of me. She and I had already spoken about Jack's sudden change earlier while we made breakfast for Fi's little ones, then sent them off to school. Fiona's housekeeper, who made many of the family meals and kept an eye on the children while my sister worked, had a week off so that she could visit her sister in Denver. Bad timing. But that's what sisters were for. We were here for Fiona and always would be.

Mama began talking about the first time she had met the little French twins. "They were adorable and we couldn't understand a thing they said. Once we got them over here, though, they quickly adapted. Soon, they seemed the same as the rest of the children here in town."

We were interrupted when Li appeared in the doorway. Pale and shaky seeming, Li's hair was disheveled, and a shadow of a beard covered his chin. I'd never seen him looking anything but perfectly groomed. He wore a pair of trousers with just an undershirt. Had he slept at all? Probably not.

"Li, dearest. What can we do for you?" Mama set her knitting aside to go to him and gather him into an embrace. He seemed to crumple into her. His grandmother had passed five or so years ago. The only blood family he had left was his sister Fai, who lived in Chicago with her husband and family. Since then, he'd grown even closer to my mother and father.

After a moment, Li stepped out of Mama's embrace. "Delphia, she wants to see you."

I started. "Me?" I'd not thought it would be me she would ask for, assuming it would be Mama or Cym.

Li put his hands in his pocket and dipped his chin. "She wants to hear stories about Bleu from when you were kids and in high school. It would give her great comfort to hear your tales about those times. He and Beaumont adored you and Jack."

"The four of us were thick as thieves," I said, standing. "I'm grateful for the time with him." Tears were hot under my eyelids, wanting to spring forth, but I kept it together. I must be strong for Li and my sister.

I followed Li up the stairs. Their home was large and spacious, with tall ceilings and wainscoting along the walls and stairwells. They'd had it built ten years back when their family started growing, leaving the cottage for their housekeeper and her husband, who took care of the gardens. Li and Fiona had done well for themselves, composing pieces for moving pictures. This house was their pride and joy because it had given the adopted twins and their little ones a real home.

Fiona was curled up in a chair by the window in their bedroom. The curtains were drawn, leaving the room in virtual darkness. I went to her, sitting on the ottoman next to her. "I'm here, Fi. What can I do?"

She lifted her gaze to me. "Tell me the funniest stories. Anything that tells me how well he lived while he was here on earth. That he was joyful and loved." She brought a hanky up to her mouth and stared at me from her red eyes.

"I have so many," I said. "Where should I start?"

I didn't wait for her to answer, beginning with the story from our graduation night when the boys had insisted on climbing up the ski mountain to watch the stars and lights of town. "We had a blanket, which Jack had thought of, always practical, you know. And I'd sneaked a bottle of wine from Papa's cellar. I was terrible, wasn't I?"

"You were young and adventurous," Fiona said kindly.

"Anyway, we were sipping away and talking about all the things we wanted to do with our lives. I had college around the corner. Jack said he wanted to breed the best racehorse that ever lived. Beaumont wanted to make pretty structures that would last. Bleu's dream was simpler. He said he wanted to make you and Li proud and pay you back for taking them home with you and giving them a family and love and safety. He planned on becoming a great success to show you that you'd made the right choice to rescue him."

Fiona dabbed at her eyes. "He was always such a sweet boy. He'd already paid us back by being such a loving and dutiful son."

"I don't know if this will soothe your broken heart or not," I said. "But he was the most joyful, thankful person I've ever known. Every day was a gift to him. He breathed in every moment of his life, enjoying everything that came his way. Did you ever hear the story about when they took the rowboat down the river and got stuck in the rocks?"

She shook her head. "Tell me."

For the next few hours, I told her as many of the stories as I could recall from my years of friendship with Bleu. There were tears and laughter and so much love in the room that I knew Bleu was there with us. Our loved ones' physical bodies may not be on earth but their souls linger, watching out for us and sending warmth and guidance in ways we will never truly understand. Until, one day, it will be our turn and we'll be reunited in heaven. All our questions will be answered then. For now, I would love those still here with every bit of my heart.

21

JACK

The days after the news of Bleu's death were hard for all of us. I had moments of despair and sadness and sudden ones of a memory that made me smile or laugh. Through it all, he felt close to me, almost guiding me toward the right path.

A week after we learned of his death, I asked my father to pick me up at the house and take me out to see Cymbeline and Viktor. Papa left me and said he'd be back after a quick jaunt into town for supplies. I thanked him and headed down the shoveled walkway to the front porch.

Cym answered the door wearing tweed trousers and a man's shirt. She held a wooden spoon in her hand, and a sprinkling of flour smeared her chin. "Jack, what are you doing here?" She smiled in a rather smug fashion, obviously knowing exactly why I was here.

"I'm here to see about training for a competition against myself," I said.

"Excellent. Come in. I'm sorry for my appearance. I've been making Christmas cakes and pies for the festival. We're auctioning them off to raise money for a few of the families in need. Husbands are off at the war, and their young wives are struggling to make ends meet and raise kids all by themselves."

Our annual Christmas festival was tomorrow. I'd forgotten about it entirely what with all the other things going on in my life. The scents of cinnamon and butter tickled my nose the moment I walked into the house.

"Making cakes without much sugar has proven to be a challenge," Cym said. "However, I used some of the honey from our bees, and I think they've turned out very nicely."

"It smells wonderful."

"Would you care for tea or coffee?" Cym asked, motioning toward the kitchen. "I need to check on the cakes, but we can talk in the kitchen."

I followed her long strides across the living room. My crutches were still a hindrance, but I was getting faster. Trying to keep up with Cym was a good test. The kitchen was decorated in greens and yellows. They'd put in one of the updated kitchen models that had become popular before the war. Viktor and Cym's sporting goods shop did very well, even with the hiccups provided by the war. Cym's competitions had brought in tidy sums back in the day as well, but she was retired from all that now.

"What are you doing these days to keep out of trouble?" I asked, teasing.

"That's a good question. Since my forced retirement because I'm getting too darned old, I have found a few new escapades to keep my attention. They've let me start a girls' athletic program at the high school. I'm teaching them to ski this winter and training them in softball come spring. It's about time, if you ask me."

"Don't all the girls here know how to ski?" I asked.

"Sliding down the mountain like your hair's on fire is not skiing," Cym said. "I teach them proper skills. It's so much fun."

Her pretty face lit up. "My goal is for the girls to beat the boys' teams in whatever it is we choose to play."

"Good luck with that."

She waved a wooden spoon at me. "Don't think I can't do it."

"I've no doubt." I laughed. "Just don't beat me with that thing. I come in peace."

"You're looking better than the last time I saw you. Less like a bum."

"A good haircut and shave will do wonders." I leaned one crutch against the table and lowered myself into a chair. "I'm hoping you can assist me further in my transformation. I'd like to start training with you—if the offer still stands."

"Yes, absolutely. You'll have to come to the school, though. We can use the gymnasium before classes start. Will that work for you?"

I had to think about this for a moment. How would I get there? I couldn't drive myself.

"I'll pick you up and take you home," Cym said. The Barnes women had an uncanny way of reading one's mind.

"That would be wonderful. Thank you."

"What made you change your mind?"

I had a feeling she already knew, but I answered anyway. "I want to be worthy of your sister. Sitting around feeling sorry for myself was not the way to do that."

"You're a good man, Jack, who's had it hard. No one blames you for a little self-pity. I knew you'd snap out of it."

"I'm trying." I studied the black-and-white kitchen tiles. "Bleu's death...I can't let it be in vain."

"May he rest in peace." Cym glanced upward, toward heaven.

A shiver went through me. Bleu was up there watching, I was sure of it. I'd made him proud.

"We can start tomorrow," Cym said. "Now, how about a cup of coffee and a piece of cake? One split in half when I took it out of the oven and someone has to eat it."

196

"I can't say no to that." I grinned back at her. Good old Cymbeline. It didn't take much to get back on her good side, and I was glad to be here.

———————————

As promised, Cymbeline appeared at my doorstep right at seven the next morning wearing tan overalls over a checkered shirt. Her hair was pulled back in a red bandanna.

"Morning," she said brightly. "Are you ready?"

"As much as I'm able." I lifted one crutch for emphasis. I'd dressed in my marine fatigues, figuring they were best for physical training. They'd been good enough for the United States Marines, anyway. "Am I wearing the right clothes?" I looked downward, catching sight of the tied pant leg where my right leg used to be.

"You'll do," Cym said. "Now come on. I've got things to do later."

"Yes, ma'am."

An hour later, I was lying on the floor of the newly built high school gymnasium, sweaty, limp, and still panting. I might hate Cym a little. She was as ferocious as any of the drill sergeants I'd come in contact with.

I sat up and scooted over to rest my back against the wall. The rope, attached to a ceiling beam, seemed to mock me, still swaying slightly from my efforts. My new nemesis, this rope. Cym had informed me that one goal was to be able to climb to the top and back down again. It was not easy to do with both legs and nearly impossible, given my weakened upper body, with one. She assured me that after a month I'd be climbing it with no problems whatsoever. I doubted it but didn't want to argue. Not with her.

Regardless, I'd made it less than a foot today. My hands and arms ached from the effort. In addition to the rope, I'd endured

TESS THOMPSON

sit-ups, lifting a bag of flour overhead, using canned beans for bicep curls, and push-ups, of which I could only do two. It was difficult to balance on only one foot. Cym assured me that with more practice, my body and brain would become used to it and I'd be fit once more.

If she'd seen me at the height of my strength. I'd done sixty push-ups one morning in a contest with one of my buddies, Tex. He'd done sixty-four, and I'd only made it to sixty. He and the others gave me a lot of good-natured grief about it. This was before we shipped out and realized how foolish it was to care about who could do more push-ups when we were about to face death. Tex died right in front of me two weeks after we got to the South Pacific. His upper body strength was no good against a grenade.

In addition, Cym had me doing one-legged squats while holding on to a balance beam with my right hand for support.

She plopped down on the floor next to me. "I was nothing but a pool of sweat that first day Viktor trained me. He had me tossing rocks around and running sprints—all terrible. I remember questioning if any of it would make a bit of difference in my jumps. But after a few weeks, my body adjusted, and then I started looking forward to those mornings. Of course, I was also falling in love with Viktor at the same time, so that added to the experience. When I went back to the slopes, all the hard work had done what it should. I felt invincible."

"I wish I could feel that way again. Leaving here, I naively thought I was too tough to get hurt over there. What an idiot."

"You had to think that way, otherwise it would be too scary to go." Cym rested her head against the wall of the gym. Her legs were spread out long on the floor, as if we were lounging by the side of the river. "No one can be courageous without a little belief in themselves."

"Even if it's false," I said.

"Especially then."

"How's Fiona holding up?" I asked.

"She's...broken. That's the only way I can describe it. I wish there were something I could do, but the grief of a mother has no cure, not even time. She's always been the kindest and most pure-hearted of all of us. I mean, look at what she did, bringing the twins back with her. Most twenty-year-olds wouldn't have done such a thing."

"It was remarkable."

"We're all capable of great bravery and fortitude, or the human race wouldn't have survived this long. Fiona will find a way to keep going. That's what we do. Just as you are right now. Choosing to come here today and fight for your life and marriage, it's the real measure of who you are. I see who you are, Jack Depaul, and I'm proud to count you as my brother."

My eyes stung. "I'm thankful for you as well. This is generous of you. I know I was awful to you when I first got home."

"Forget about that. What you've been through—it's not for sissies. You're deserving of a little grace and forgiveness, especially from yourself."

"Thanks, Cym."

"You're welcome. Now, are you ready to get up? I have to get home to get the girls off to school."

"Yes ma'am."

She jumped up and offered me a hand, helping me to my feet and supporting my weight while handing me my crutches. "Phillip wants to try his hand on a prosthetic. You should do it. Learn to walk with it and take your wife dancing."

"You think it's possible?"

"I do. I have faith in yourself and Phillip and God. Sometimes that's all we have."

"Yes, ma'am."

FOR AT LEAST THE hundredth time since I'd been home, I was thankful for the shower Delphia had cleverly installed. While the hot water ran over me, I closed my eyes for a moment to enjoy the feel of it on my skin. I'd become fairly adept at leaning on my one crutch and washing my hair and body with the other hand. In fact, I was feeling quite pleased with myself. That must have been my mistake, because I slipped getting out and fell. Perhaps it was because my muscles were tired from the exercise and I'd let my mind drift to thoughts of my wife in our bed the night before. Whatever the reason, I crashed to the floor and onto my backside without warning.

My tailbone hurt, but other than that I was all right. I sat there on the floor for a good five minutes until the chill of the room made it impossible to do. First, I wrapped a towel around my waist. Then, using the bar on the wall, I managed to get myself up and pull both crutches under my arms.

Once inside the bedroom, I sat on the bed and donned the flannel bathrobe I'd set there earlier. The fall had shaken me. Just when I thought I was starting to improve mentally and physically, the reality of my new world pushed its way into my consciousness.

I lay back against the pillows, even though the bed had already been made by my clever wife, and pulled a throw blanket over myself. The doctors had told me to rest if and when I wanted. For once in my life, I didn't fight. I closed my eyes and slept.

When I woke, it was to the noise of Delphia's heels clicking up the stairs. She burst into the room a second later, her eyes wild. "Are you all right?" She rushed to my side. "I called earlier and there was no answer and I got worried so I came home. Are you ill?"

I rolled to my left side and smiled. "I'm fine. You look like an angel." She did, too, with her blond hair and blue eyes that matched her wool coat. Her fair skin glowed from the cold under the rim of her knit cloche hat.

She sat down next to me and stroked my hair. "Why are you in bed?"

"Your sister wore me out. And I fell getting out of the shower."

Her forehead wrinkled in worry as her gaze traveled the length of my body. "Did you hurt anything?"

"My tailbone's a little sore, but nothing serious."

"We need a better pad in the shower. Something rough that's hard to slip on. I'll figure something out."

"You always do, my darling girl."

She narrowed her eyes, scrutinizing me. "You seem different."

"Different how?"

"Peaceful maybe? I don't know exactly." She ran her hand down my shoulder and along my arm. "And so very handsome."

"You know, these naps during the day could include some-thing else." I let my eyes twinkle up at her.

"Mr. Depaul, are you suggesting what I think you're suggesting?"

I rolled onto my back. "Come on in and see for yourself."

22

DELPHIA

Somehow, our family got through the next few months. Fiona was devastated, as we knew she would be. Li, too, seemed to be in a fog of grief. It was only their music and their young children that kept them going. A month after we learned of Bleu's death, they began to work on an orchestra piece to honor their adopted son. "Our opus," Fiona said to me one night as we sat side by side in my parents' formal living room after a family Sunday dinner.

Christmas had passed without the celebrations of years past. We were all somber and worried, faking it only for the children. During the bleak days of January, we all forged on, as did the rest of the country. As sad as I was about Bleu, and he was never far from my thoughts, I was thankful that Jack seemed to be doing better with each passing day.

He'd taken Cym up on her offer to train him back into shape. Although he didn't tell me much about it, I could see his muscles returning as well as the color to his cheeks. He headed to Cym's right after breakfast and returned a few hours later, red-faced and sweaty. "Your sister's a beast," he said to me at the end of the first week.

I fed him as best I could with my new cooking skills, and his face lost the gaunt, hollow look. He'd not said anything further about using a prosthetic, and I didn't want to bring up the subject for fear it would upset him. Whatever he wanted to do, it should be his choice. He'd grown so adept with his crutches, bounding up the stairs and around the house, that I suspected he might not want the prosthetic at all.

I continued working at the club and volunteering for the war efforts, but I'd cut down my hours at both. The newly hired bartender ran the club during the evenings, supervising the staff and interacting with customers, and I took care of the business aspects of ordering and keeping the books. Profits were down. All the men were at war, and women were too tired from working full-time jobs to go out much. Despite all that, we were fine financially, even if we had to be frugal. I'd have preferred if Jack worked with his father out at the farm, but thus far he'd not said anything about doing so. Again, I didn't push him. I figured he'd come to his own conclusions about work, too. He'd said only that he was useless to his father as long as he was attached to his crutches. If he didn't want to work at his family's business, I wondered what he would do. If I were to ever become pregnant, he would have to find a job. Still, I kept my mouth shut. For now, I was happy that he seemed to be returning to his prior robustness.

One morning in the spring of 1943, I woke to the sound of birds singing outside the windows and bright sunlight peeking through the shades. I grabbed my robe and went to the window, drawing back the curtains. Blinking in the bright light, I took a moment to look out to our property. All the snow had melted and the meadows were filled with wildflowers and the fruit trees surrounding our house blossomed pink and white. Green grasses sparkled with morning dew. What a beautiful sight, I thought. Spring, with its promise of renewal, had arrived after the long months of winter.

I showered and dressed and went downstairs. Jack had already left for his training session with Cym. Usually, she dropped him back by around nine, and it was not yet eight. I made coffee and was about to fry an egg when the postman came by.

To my surprise, it was a letter from Beaumont. I quickly looked at the postal date. It was sent after we'd learned of Bleu. With shaking hands, I used my silver letter opener to slice through the top of the envelope.

Dear Jack and Delphia,

They informed me about Bleu, but it doesn't seem real. I'm sorry about your leg, Jack, but glad you're home. I hope I get out of here alive so my mother doesn't have to suffer further. Some nights the only thing that gets me through is memories of when we were kids. I wish we could go back in time and live them all again.

I thought I would have felt when Bleu left this earth, being his twin and all. I didn't. And now I just feel this black emptiness, like I fell into an inkwell.

I'm somewhere with so much mud it's all we see and feel and taste. Our boots are no good either. It's endless, this walking and walking. My feet are cold all the time and I'm afraid to take the boots off for fear I can't put them back on since they're swollen.

Anyway, I love you both. Please look after my mom for me.

Beaumont

I wiped away the tears that dampened my cheeks. Walking and walking with boots that didn't provide protection? Was this really the best we could do for our boys?

Where was he? My guess was Italy. Our troops were marching north, freeing villages along the way. How long would it go on?

I set the letter aside and wept for Bleu and Beaumont and of course Jack. The night before our wedding flashed before my eyes. We'd all been hopeful then. Everything had changed.

I was still crying when Jack came in through the kitchen door. "Hey, what's wrong?"

I gestured toward the envelope. "It's from Beaumont."

He picked it up and read it quickly. "He sounds bad."

"Yes." I nodded and wiped my face. "There's nothing to do but forge on. What do you want for supper?"

"I have a surprise for you," Jack said. "I'm taking you out to dinner."

"You are?"

"At the lodge. And then I have another treat after that. Put on your prettiest dress."

Although my spirits wished otherwise, I did as he asked. Forging on.

I wore my blue chiffon dress. It had sat in the closet since I'd worn it last, a night of celebration when I graduated from Bryn Mawr. How long ago that seemed. I'd been young then, and now I'd aged years and years.

Standing in front of the full-length mirror near my dressing table, I thought I looked all right. It was looser around my waist and hips than it once was. All the girls wanted to be thin back at school. We hadn't had any idea what was coming, or we would have enjoyed all the cake.

But all in all, I didn't look too bad. I had gone into town to have my hair set, and it shone under the lights. Behind me, Jack walked through the bedroom door. He took my breath away in the black suit he'd worn at our wedding. It took me a moment to notice that his right pant leg was not tied up as he usually had it. And he didn't have his crutches. He had on two shoes and leaned on a beautiful wooden cane. "Jack?"

He grinned. "I've been working on a little project with Phillip.

He's made a prosthetic. Much better than the one issued by the hospital. I won't be able to wear it all the time, but I can tonight." He lifted his pant leg. There, where his leg should have been, was a delicately carved piece of wood attached to what looked a bit like a pincushion. It was a work of art, mimicking the size and shape of his other leg very well. Even the foot must be the right size, because it seemed to fit in the shoe perfectly. At the top of the artificial limb, a hole had been carved out, leaving the sides to surround his real leg. "He put a lever in so that it mimics the knee."

"It's…I don't even know what to say. Phillip's a genius."

"He truly is. And he has the patience of Job. Do you know how long it took him to carve this?"

"I can only imagine."

"Well, his hard work has given me a chance to take you dancing after dinner. I've been practicing. So let's get going. We have a new memory to make."

He could not twirl me as he once had, but he could put one arm around me while holding on to the cane with the other. I didn't care about the lack of movement. Who needed to go from one end of the dance floor to the other anyway? I was close to him. He had his arm around me while standing. It was better than I'd ever hoped for.

"Are people staring at me?" Jack asked in my ear.

"I've no idea. All I know is that I'm staring at you."

Over the last few months, he'd filled out and his muscular frame had returned, thanks to my sister. I knew every inch of him now. His muscles rippled under my touch every night.

"I'm going out to see my papa tomorrow," Jack said. "I want to show him this new leg of mine and see if I can get back on a horse."

"Jack, that would be wonderful."

206

"Thank you for staying with me," Jack said. "I'll try to make it up to you in the years we have left."

"I hope there are many many more like today."

We danced to a few more songs, but my feet were getting blisters in the high heels I hadn't worn since before the war. I worried the skin on his stump might be doing the same. "Let's go home, my darling," I whispered in his ear. "What I have in mind will not require an upright position."

He laughed. "I will follow you anywhere, but especially there."

"We're lucky, you know that?"

He pulled me closer and kissed me. "I do. I truly do."

23

QUINN

I 'd lived in Emerson Pass for almost three decades when we learned the war had ended. Germany had surrendered in early May of 1945, followed by the Japanese in September. We waited anxiously for the news that the boys from our small part of the world would return to those who loved them. By Christmas of 1945, our wishes had been granted. Beaumont, James, and Theo were all home for the holiday.

I worried about Fiona for months and months after we learned of Bleu's death. She was not herself, growing so thin I thought she might blow away in one of our blizzards. Although it was true that she would never get over the loss of her boy, over time, she began to live again. The haunting of his death was reflected only in the new sadness in her eyes and in the heartbreaking notes of her music.

She and Li had grown closer than ever. I noticed him watching her, always sure to be there if she needed any little thing. His stoic expression never changed, but I could see in his eyes, too, that he suffered along with his wife. He'd told Alexander not long ago that the desire to protect his wife from further pain was one of the main motivators of his life. "I will do anything for her, to ease her burden," he'd said. "Yet I find it's impossible to make up for the loss of her child. Still, I do my best to cherish her and be there when she needs to weep the tears that only a mother who has lost a son or daughter can know."

His devotion broke my heart in the best way.

Today, Fiona and I had stolen away for a quick chat upstairs in what had once been the bedroom she'd shared with her sisters, long before Addie and Delphia had blessed our lives. I could remember the three little beds exactly as they'd been when I first came to them. The ghosts of their laughter still echoed there in the rafters. Perhaps only I could hear it?

Fiona had sat on the edge of the bed where grandchildren now came to stay for overnight visits. She wore a modest red dress, perfect for Christmas. Silver had come to a few strands of her hair, and she'd promptly decided to dye them away. They were like her grief, not visible but there just the same.

"Darling, how are you?" I asked, sitting next to her and taking her hand. "I worry. Especially this time of year."

"I'm fine, Mama." She tilted her head to rest her cheek against my shoulder. "My little ones help. I can remember feeling a little sick when we found out I was pregnant again after the first two and with the twins being teenagers. 'All these children,' I'd said to Li. 'How will we support them?' He'd only smiled and said not to worry. God always came through. I've thought about that many times since. The ways the Lord works are mysterious to me, but I have to surrender to faith. Some days it's all I have to hold on to."

"And family," I said softly. "We're always here for you."

"I know, Mama. For that, I am always grateful." She looked out the window where fat Christmas flakes blanketed the ground in white. "I know I'll see him again."

"Yes, just as I'll see my mother and father."

"I had a dream the other night about Bleu. In it, I was in the rocking chair in the nursery. I had a baby boy in my arms. I knew he was Bleu even though I never knew him when he was that small. But then, I looked up to see him standing in the doorway. He was smiling and wearing the suit he wore to Delphia's wedding. He looked so handsome and peaceful and then he said, 'I'm here with my maman, so don't worry about me. We're keeping each other company until the rest of you arrive.' I woke up, in tears, and wishing I could see him one more time."

"Perhaps you will," I said. "In your dreams, I mean."

"Yes. He was always such a sweet little boy, concerned for others. The dream gave me such a feeling of...surrender...I guess you would say. He's there with his mother. That's enough, isn't it? To know that?"

"It doesn't mean you don't ache for him, though. As only a mother can."

"I used to wonder if you ever hesitated to take us all on," Fiona said. "But when I met the twins, I knew exactly how you'd felt."

"Like you belonged to me and I to you."

"Yes, just like that."

Jo appeared in the doorway then, knocking softly. "Are you two hiding from Santa in here?" She smiled, but concern glinted in her eyes. "Papa was wondering where you were. I told him I'd check up here. Is everything all right?" She came to stand near the bed. Wearing a silky blue dress and with her hair pulled back with silver barrettes, she looked very much like the girl I'd first met, even though fine lines around her mouth and eyes hinted at her age. It seemed she'd finally caught up to the age she'd always been in her head.

"Oh, yes, Jo, we're just fine," Fiona said. "Having a little bit of a moment."

"As you should," Jo said, sitting in the rocking chair.

"Christmas is always hard since we lost Bleu. There's no reason to be ashamed."

"Thanks, Jo," Fiona said. "I hope someday I can face Christmas without feeling so melancholy."

I squeezed her hand and kissed her temple. She might be in her thirties, but she was still my little princess girl. "You're doing very well, darling. We're all so proud of you."

Cym and Delphia showed up next, followed by Addie, all three looking lovely and excited. As tough as Cym was, she delighted in Christmas. Delphia glowed with happiness. She was pregnant with her second child, due in the spring. Addie's color and spark had returned since James had come home. Tonight, she had a certain incandescence about her.

"Come in and sit with us a moment," I said. "It's seldom I have all my girls together at the same time these days."

"Yes, Mama," Addie said, always obedient.

Cym wrapped her arms around the bedpost. Addie and Delphia sat together in the oversize leather chair.

"Papa has all the kids together downstairs," Cym said. "He's reading *The Night Before Christmas*. It's enough to make even the least sentimental of us cry."

"My girls look forward to that every year," Jo said. "Even though they're grown women in their twenties." It was hard to believe that Poppy and Quinn were adults, ready to begin their lives. Poppy, Jo's oldest daughter, had gone to college and decided to stay back east. Fortunately, she and her fiancé were here for Christmas. Quinn, my namesake, was finishing up her college degree at a university in New England. She was home for the holiday as well, mooning over a beau she'd left behind.

"Your father loves every minute of it." The tradition had started with Josephine's girls and had been carried out every year since.

"Speaking of my girls," Jo said, "Quinn's in love. She thinks her young man's going to propose when she graduates in the spring."

"Not without meeting us first," Cym said. "We have to approve of him."

Josephine laughed. "Her father said the same thing. She's planning on bringing him out here after graduation. He wants to ask Phillip's permission."

"What if he says no?" Delphia asked.

"Don't be silly. Phillip's too kindhearted to do such a thing," Addie said. "Unless the man's truly awful."

"Which he won't be," Cym said. "I'd be surprised if Quinn had poor taste in husbands. She has all of ours as good examples of what to look for."

"How true," Addie said.

I glanced over at Addie. She looked almost plump. Her belly seemed rounded under the material of her evening dress. Was that the reason for her glow? Dare I dream? Was she going to have a baby at long last?

"I hope he won't have a reason to say no," Jo said. "Wouldn't that be awful?"

"Let's not borrow trouble," I said. "Quinn has probably picked a wonderful young man. She's very wise for her age." I turned to Addie. "You're looking well, darling. Anything you want to share with us?"

Addie blushed, then giggled. "As a matter of fact, I do. I'm going to have a baby. Due this summer, if Louisa's calculations are correct."

"Oh, darling, really?" I asked. Addie had been brave about it, but I knew she wanted a baby. She'd never have admitted it to us, for fear we would worry.

"Can you believe it? After all this time?" Addie beamed at me. "James is beside himself, even though he says he's going to be an old dad."

"James seems young though," Fiona said. "Young at heart. He'll make a wonderful father."

"Even the war and everything he saw over there hasn't changed him," Addie said. "He's still as sweet and kind as ever. The students at school will be so happy to have him come back."

"Is he excited to get back to teaching?" Josephine asked.

"Yes, he is. After a few more months of rest, though. He won't be returning until next autumn." Addie's brow creased. "I had to convince him that it was all right to take a break. We're doing fine because of my books, you know." She flushed, looking embarrassed. "I'm sorry. I don't mean to sound like a braggart."

"Don't be silly," Cym said. "You're a star, just like we knew you would be."

"We are very proud of you," I said.

A lump developed in the back of my throat. My two youngest were both rosy from pregnancy and in good health. *Thank you, Lord*, I prayed silently. *Thank you for keeping us all safe.*

"I'm proud of all of you." My eyes stung with joy and gratitude. "I'm so very lucky to be your mother."

"Whether it's a boy or a girl, we're going to name the baby Bleu," Addie said. "In honor of our dear Bleu."

Fiona's eyes grew glassy. "That's lovely. Li and Beaumont will be so pleased. As am I."

"I think a little girl Bleu would be adorable," Cym said. "Maybe she'll be a tomboy like her auntie."

"We already have one of those," Fiona said, referring to her young child, a little girl named Cassandra, whom we all called Cassie. "She came out of the womb kicking, if you recall, and hasn't stopped yet. She takes after Cym if there ever was one."

"It's strange how things work, isn't it?" Cym said. "My Holly's musical like you and your daughter's athletic like me. Isn't it grand?"

"It's perfectly perfect," Fiona said, exchanging a sweet smile with her sister.

"As long as he or she comes out healthy, we don't care which we have," Addie said.

"Amen to that," Jo said.

I looked around the room at the beautiful faces of my daughters, hoping I would never forget how they looked at this moment. How blessed I'd been in motherhood. The hard times and periods of worry had faded from my mind, leaving me with only sweet memories. For a moment, I saw them as they'd been when they were little girls. How innocent and sweet they'd been. I wished they'd never had to suffer as Fiona had, but that was not up to me. God had a plan for all of us. My faith remained intact, even in the face of Fiona's grief.

Shannon and Louisa came into the bedroom. "Sorry we're late," Louisa said, cheeks flushed and strands of hair falling attractively across her forehead. Since the discovery of midwifery, her true calling—all these years ago now—she'd come into her own. There wasn't a woman in town who didn't trust her to aid in the delivery of their babies and rightly so. Over the years, she'd continued to learn the most modern techniques for labor and delivery. She rarely lost a baby, and then it was something out of her control. Still, she grieved those lost babies almost as hard as their mother. She truly cared for her patients and their babies. It was no secret why she was so beloved.

"I had to deliver a baby boy for Mrs. O'Brien," Louisa said. "He's a jolly, fat little man with a giant noggin." She gestured with her hands to show us the size of the baby's head. If it were as wide as indicated, poor Mrs. O'Brien. I would send her a basket of food tomorrow morning.

"He took forever to make his grand entrance," Louisa said, plopping down next to me. "I'm dead on my feet. Thank goodness both my boys are home. They promised to take care of Christmas breakfast tomorrow morning so that I could sleep late. Aren't they the dearest?" Theo, who had performed his duties as a war doctor without complaint, was now back where he belonged, taking care of the people of Emerson Pass. Their son, Simon, who had been called up shortly after he turned eighteen in 1943, had become a medic, following in his father's footsteps. Fortunately, he'd been spared combat and saved countless lies. Simon was a gentle, sensitive soul like his father. Strangely enough, since he had no blood in common with our dear departed Simon Lind, he reminded me of Louisa's adopted father. I'd suspected he might follow the path of a pastor, but medicine won his affection instead. He'd announced yesterday that he intended to go to medical school to become a doctor like both his parents. I knew he'd rely on God as part of his healing practice, as Louisa and Theo did.

"And I had to deliver the last of the pies," Shannon said. "Not as dramatic as a baby, of course, but hopefully enough to cheer those who need it." Every year she made dozens of pies and delivered them on Christmas Eve to families who were struggling financially.

"You haven't missed a thing," I said, wishing the moment could last just a little longer. "But I'm glad to see all of you together in the same room. All my beauties."

"I love you to pieces, and Flynn and I are as excited as the children today," Shannon said, stooping to kiss my cheek. She was pretty in a silver evening dress with her black curls coaxed into the tamer style of the day. "All our boys home and all of us together. It's a dream come true. My mother's on her way over with Rand. She said they might be a few minutes late as they wanted to stop and see Rand's daughter and new baby on the way." Shannon's mother, Moira, after many years of widowhood, had been remarried five or so years ago to a nice man named Rand Harding. He owned the barbershop and was well-liked by all. We were pleased to see Moira spend her golden years happily married.

"Well," I said, standing. "As much as I've enjoyed this, we should all go downstairs. It's time for a little Christmas punch while we wait for Moira and Rand."

"Before we go downstairs," Josephine said, rising to her feet as well. "Mama, we have a gift for you. We all pitched in to get it for you." She pulled a small box from her pocket and handed it to me.

"This is such a treat," I said, delighted. "But I don't need a thing."

"Just open it, Mama." Delphia grinned mischievously.

I untied the ribbon and lifted the lid from the box. Inside was a silver cross encased in small diamonds on a delicate chain. "Girls, this is too much. It must have cost you a fortune."

"We all contributed," Addie said. "Like you taught us, we can do anything together."

"Would you like me to help fasten it?" Cym asked.

I stood, handing the necklace to Cym. "Yes. Won't it look lovely with my dress?"

"Mama, you always look lovely," Fiona said. "You always have and you always will, because it comes from the inside out."

"To think, all this time I thought I was plain," I said, laughing. I had thought that before I met Alexander. Once I saw myself reflected in his eyes, I knew the capacity of my beauty. He made me feel that way, regardless of what the mirror told me. Over the years, I'd discovered the mirror lies to us anyway. All it shows are our flaws when to human eyes other than our own, especially those who love us, only our beauty is apparent. I wanted to tell my girls this discovery, but they were all sweeping around me, embracing me and saying how much they loved me, and I was too overcome to give them one of my mama lessons.

But perhaps they already knew this truth. They had men at

their sides who thought their wife the most beautiful woman in the world. Even before that, their dear papa had looked at them in a way that could only be interpreted one way. They were perfection in his eyes. *Perfectly perfect.* Was this the secret to raising secure, strong women who knew their value?

We all traipsed downstairs, chattering and laughing. The Barnes clan would never be accused of being too quiet. When we reached the bottom of the stairwell, I gasped at the sight before me. It was my sister, Annabelle, and her husband, Bromley, standing in the foyer, taking off coats and wraps. She squealed when she saw me, as did I. "My baby sister? Am I really seeing you?" Annabelle had spent most of the war years in Florida with her husband and his family. They'd married a few years after our sweet Clive had left us to meet his maker. We all adored Bromley and his old-fashioned manners and sunny disposition. The two of them had been very happy together for years now, but we all still referred to him as her new husband.

"We decided to surprise you," Annabelle said. "Just like that first Christmas. Do you remember?"

"How could I ever forget?" Alexander had sent for Annabelle and our mother so that they might be with me on our wedding day. They'd become proud residents of Emerson Pass the moment they'd stepped off the train. As had I.

We hugged and cried and clung to each other for a bit before I withdrew to greet Bromley. He kissed my hand in his gallant way and thanked me for the invitation to dinner. "She's my sister and thus you are my brother," I said. "And we couldn't be happier to see you both."

The entire lot of us meandered into the sitting room. Although the parlor was meant for holiday gatherings, somehow we always ended up in our less formal room. So much had happened here over the years. I could almost hear the echoes of the declarations of love and first kisses and sisterly bickering. Now it was a roar of laughter and everyone talking at once, punctuated by the sound of music coming from Fiona and her piano and Li's violin. Most of the grandchildren had gathered around to sing Christmas carols, mostly off-key, but Fiona didn't seem to mind.

The fire warmed the room. One of the maids, who I'd offered double pay to work Christmas Eve, sailed around the room delivering punch and ciders to the children. The men all partook of Alexander's whiskey. Some of my girls enjoyed sherry, but I preferred to drink what the children drank. I almost laughed, remembering how I'd nearly choked that first night I'd arrived. Alexander had thought it so funny. I'd declared never to try whiskey again, and I'd kept that promise.

My gaze scanned the room. For the first time since before the war, we'd cut down a Christmas tree for the sitting room. Decorated with strings of red cranberries and ornaments the children had made over the years, its spicy scent filled the room. Alexander had brought home a string of electric lights and wrapped them around the branches. They made me ridiculously happy.

Viktor and Cym were cozied up in one of the wide-back armchairs, whispering about something or other. Addie and Delphia sat side by side, their pregnant bellies touching, talking closely. Delphia's little girl, named Adelaide but whom we all called Leddie, was sound asleep against her mother's chest. She was only eighteen months and tiny for her age, just as Delphia had been. The first time I'd held Leddie, I'd been transformed back in time to the birth of my Delphia. They looked so alike it was uncanny. Everything was a circle, I thought now, that seemed to return to the same place again and again.

Addie's and Delphia's husbands, who had become the best of friends despite their age difference, were playing a lively game of checkers on the couch opposite their wives. James looked toward me, perhaps feeling my gaze. I smiled at him as he rose to his feet to embrace me. "Cheers, my American mother. Are you keeping well enough?" James asked in my ear.

"I've never been better, dear James." I placed my hands on the sides of his fine face. "I'm so happy about the baby."

"Me too. I'd resigned myself to otherwise, but I'm grateful God had other plans," James said. "A Christmas miracle, don't you think?"

"I certainly do. You deserve a few miracles," I said. "After serving our country so well."

"Ah, it was nothing. Writing about the war was easy considering what most of the boys went through."

"I know your newspaper gave the troops something to look forward to," I said. "That's nothing to be humble about." His contribution to the army newspaper had earned him the love and respect of many, many men.

Jack had risen up from the sofa with only the aid of his cane. Since the success of his prosthetic, he and Phillip were obsessed with refining it to fit better and better. Other than the cane, one would never guess at the trauma and pain the poor boy had endured. He was strong now and as wide as three men, thanks to Cym's brutal training regimen. "You're looking awfully well," I said to him. "As if you could lift the house with one arm."

"Or one leg, as the case may be," Jack said, laughing. "Cym's tougher on me than the Marine Corps. But thank you."

Louisa and Shannon had both managed to get their husbands to dance with them. Currently, they were waltzing their wives around the room to Fiona and the children singing "Joy to the World." My twin sons, still as pretty as they'd ever been, had become such strong, reliable men. A mother could not ask for more. Shannon had told me last week how the brothers had become closer than ever, spending time together with each other's families as well as alone, hiking or having a drink on a lazy evening. "They seem to have more and more to say to each other," Louisa had mentioned to me at church the week before. "The time apart made them realize how much they yearned for the other's company. They'd never really been apart before."

I nodded, knowing it was true and also happy it was so. They'd come into this world together. It was only right they spent as much of their lifetimes together as was possible.

My sister and Bromley were sitting in the corner with Jo's daughter, no doubt regaling her with tales of their adventures in Paris before the war.

Phillip approached then, holding out his hands. "May I have this dance?"

"Me? I don't know," I said.

He pulled me into his arms, waltzing me toward the fire. "You know what tonight is, don't you?"

I pretended not to, knowing what was coming. Every year on Christmas Eve, Phillip thanked me for giving him a family.

"It's my twenty-fourth year being part of this family."

I looked up at him, scarcely believing it had been that long since he'd first come through my doors. "Such a long time, darling. I think you can stop thanking me. There has to be some kind of limit to how many years you have to do so."

"Your daughter is the best thing that's ever happened to me." Phillip glanced over to the chair nearest the fire where Jo was already knitting away on a sweater for Addie's new baby. "And our two daughters—well, I could not ask for more."

"You've given more to our family than we've given you," I said. "Especially to Jack."

"That was the least I could do. It's hard to remember what he was like when he came home to us, now, though, isn't it?"

"Agreed. You helped him, and I'll never forget it."

"Excuse me, young man, but may I cut in?" It was Alexander, dapper in his best suit. My stomach fluttered, just as it had always done in his presence. We might be older, but our passion for each other was as strong as it had ever been.

"If you insist," Phillip said. "I'll see if I can tear my wife away for a Christmas dance."

He handed me over to Alexander, who took me into his arms and held me close as Fiona and the children sang "The First Noel." My favorite. Fiona knew that, of course, and smiled over at me before she began the second verse. I remembered the night so long ago when we'd all traveled into town for the winter festival, listening to Fiona sing sweetly into the cold winter's night. I could not have imagined what the years would bring, both sad and joyful, but always at the center of everything was my husband and children and grandchildren. "I'm so blessed, Alexander," I said. "Thank you for giving me this life."

"It's all you, love. Everything and everyone in this room is because of you. Your big heart and gracefulness and ability to forgive and perhaps, most of all, to see the best in all of us. You've made us all strive to be better, you know."

"You're kind to say so, but you're the rock of this family. The one who has held us together through trials and triumphs."

"If I had it to do over again, and I wish we could, I'd choose you every time."

"And I you," I said. "Always and forever."

At the end of the song, the room went silent. All the children dispersed to sit close to their parents. It was a tradition that Fiona sang "Silent Night" before we went in to dinner.

"My wife will now perform 'Silent Night,'" Li said, setting aside his violin. "And then Lizzie would like us all to head to the dining room."

I glanced over at the doorway. Jasper had his arm around Lizzie in a rare moment of stillness for both of them. My dearest friend and faithful employee, still round-cheeked and a little plumper than she once was. There was no one I trusted more in this world to take care of my family and of me. We'd convinced them to join us for dinner even though Jasper didn't like it. But with Florence back east, the holiday was hard for them. "We're your family anyway," I'd said to them earlier. "Please, this year, make an exception."

To my surprise, they'd agreed. We'd worn poor Jasper down over the years.

Fiona's pure soprano voice filled the room. If anything, her vocal ability had grown even richer than when she was a young woman. The heart and soul behind every note gave me goosebumps. I placed my cheek against my husband's chest.

Silent night, holy night...all is calm, all is bright...

I fought tears, overcome with joy by those around me but also for those who were no longer with us. My mother, Simon and Pamela Lind, our precious Mrs. Wu, sweet, sweet Bleu. The memories lingered in this room so filled with love. Those who came before us and after us were all here, even if we could not see them. For where there is love, all was possible. And with love, we never truly say goodbye. Our memories keep love alive until we reach heaven to reunite.

For now, however, I gathered Alexander closer to me, basking in the warmth of his familiar body and scent. My husband, the finest of fine men.

Fiona held one last note, and then the room exploded with clapping and cheers and gleeful anticipation of the savory meal that awaited us. As the room emptied, Alexander and I held back. When they were all gone, I turned to him.

"No one and nothing could have been better than you, my darling. This life of mine—how grand it's been."

"Aren't you glad you did it?" Alexander asked, drawing back to look into my eyes.

"Did what? Accept the teaching job?"

"Step off the train." He kissed my temple. "And into my life."

"Be brave, dear one. Your life awaits," I whispered.

He closed his eyes, smiling. "I can still see you sprawled out on the sofa. The most beautiful sight I'd ever seen. If I'd had any idea of what was to come, I wouldn't have believed it."

"Me too." I traced his bottom lip with my thumb. Wrinkles had come to the face I'd loved for so long, and yet he was the same to me as he'd always been. My love, my best friend, my destiny. "Do you remember how desperate we were for each other back then?"

"Nothing has changed in that regard, Mrs. Barnes. Only now I no longer yearn for what I can't have."

"Because you have me."

"That's correct." He bent his head and kissed me. Just like all those years ago, my breath caught.

"We'll have to save that for later," I said, laughing. "There's a Christmas roast to eat."

"I've lost my appetite." He nipped at my ear.

"You're as bad as you always were." I gave him one last kiss. "You may escort me to dinner now, Lord Barnes."

"It would be my pleasure, my lady."

On his arm, he glided me across the room and into the dining room where our family waited patiently for the original pair of lovebirds.

By this point in time, my family had grown so large we could no longer eat at one table. The children were fed downstairs in the kitchen with the nannies fussing over them and cajoling them to eat a few bites of turkey and potatoes or risk missing dessert.

I said a prayer of silent thanks for everything before me and then took my place at the head of the table. The room quieted as we bowed our heads to pray. This time, though, I kept my eyes open. My gaze drifted toward the window. Low in the sky, a star twinkled at me. Just one star. My northern light. The one that had led me home.

Home. The place where everyone I loved gathered around a table in thanks for all we had. We'd managed through hard and frightening times more than once. I hoped we never would again, but at my age, I knew that was an impossibility. Whatever came, we were here together. Nothing could steal the memory of this night. I would not even have to be brave. I had already stepped off the train. The glowing faces around my supper table were my reward.

I looked down the length of the table to my husband. His eyes sparkled and seemed to laugh at me. I blew him a kiss.

We passed around food and filled our plates and talked of Christmases past and future, but mostly of the present one for which we were so grateful.

Nights like this reminded me of the vows Alexander and I had made to each other all those years ago. Love each other with all our hearts. Leave no words of affection unsaid. Say we're sorry when we've made a mistake. Keep each other close in times of hardship. Put family above all else.

We had lived this way for many years, never breaking our promises to each other. Now, as I glanced around the room at the faces I loved so dearly, I knew without a doubt that these were the elements of a well-lived life. My life, beautiful, flawed, and yet perfectly perfect.

Step off the train, dear one. Your life awaits.

ALSO BY TESS THOMPSON

CLIFFSIDE BAY

Traded: Brody and Kara

Deleted: Jackson and Maggie

Jaded: Zane and Honor

Marred: Kyle and Violet

Tainted: Lance and Mary

Cliffside Bay Christmas, The Season of Cats and Babies (Cliffside Bay
Novella to be read after Tainted)

Missed: Rafael and Lisa

Healed: Stone and Pepper

Cliffside Bay Christmas Wedding (Cliffside Bay Novella to be read
after Healed)

Chateau Wedding (Cliffside Bay Novella to be read after Christmas
Wedding)

Scarred: Trey and Autumn

Jilted: Nico and Sophie

Kissed (Cliffside Bay Novella to be read after Jilted)

Departed: David and Sara

BLUE MOUNTAIN SERIES

Blue Mountain Bundle, Books 1,2,3

Blue Midnight

Blue Moon

Blue Ink

Blue String

EMERSON PASS

RIVER VALLEY

LEGLEY BAY

STANDALONES

ABOUT THE AUTHOR

Tess Thompson Romance...hometowns and heartstrings.

USA Today Bestselling author Tess Thompson writes small-town romances and historical romance. She started her writing career in fourth grade when she wrote a story about an orphan who opened a pizza restaurant. Oddly enough, her first novel, "Riversong" is about an adult orphan who opens a restaurant. Clearly, she's been obsessed with food and words for a long time now.

With a degree from the University of Southern California in theatre, she's spent her adult life studying story, word craft, and character. Since 2011, she's published 25 novels and 6 novellas. Most days she spends at her desk chasing her daily word count or rewriting a terrible first draft.

She currently lives in a suburb of Seattle, Washington with her husband, the hero of her own love story, and their Brady Bunch clan of two sons, two daughters and five cats. Yes, that's four kids and five cats.

Tess loves to hear from you. Drop her a line at tess@tthomp sonwrites.com or visit her website at https://tesswrites.com/

facebook.com/AuthorTessThompson
twitter.com/tesswrites
bookbub.com/authors/tess-thompson
pinterest.com/tesswrites